D1526455

He's a Bad Boy but I Love Him

Shatavia

MAY -- 2017

He's a Bad Boy but I Love Him

Copyright © 2017 by Shatavia

Published by Lucinda John Presents

All rights reserved. No part of this book may be reproduced in any form without written consent of the publisher, except brief quotes used in reviews.

This is a work of fiction. Any references or similarities to actual events, real people, living or dead, or to real locals are intended to give the novel a sense of reality. Any similarity in other names, characters, places, and incidents are entirely coincidental.family; i

Table of Contents

Chapter One

Khadijah

"Jr.! If you don't stop banging on that table you are going to get it!"

My son turned and looked at me with those big, brown eyes just like his damn father's, then walked to his bedroom and watched Bubble Guppies. Looking into my son's eyes, I could never up and leave his life without a care in the world. Yet, his father seemed to be having the time of his life, as if his son doesn't exist.

Here I was, twenty-one with a one-year-old, living on my own on the east side of Chicago. If I would have known my life was going to be this hard, I would have just avoided Kenny's ass a long time ago. I met Kenny back in high school my sophomore year; he was everything a girl in high school could ever dream of. He was loving, caring, charming, and not to mention, the first to break my v-card. After I gave myself to him, he began to distance himself from me. I should have known then to just walk away, but no, I chose to be stuck with him throughout all of his cheating and lying. Somewhere in the mix, I messed around and got pregnant.

By the time I had our son, he completely stopped coming around. Even though he's still in the area and knows where I stay, he still has not came to see his son since birth. His excuse was that he's young and he has a life, which is bullshit because he and I are the same age. It's just the mentality of a typical nigga, I guess. After that last conversation with him, I completely cut off all ties. If he chose not to be in our son's life, then so be it. After finishing up my paper for my online class, I began to start Jr.'s bath so he could get ready for bed.

Once I bathed him and put his night clothes on, he was out like a light. I kissed his forehead and closed his bedroom door, making sure I turned a nightlight on for him before I walked out. I moved into my small, two-bedroom apartment right before I had Jr. My mother was always on me about getting my own place so I wouldn't be taking up room at her house, so she helped me get this apartment and had been paying the bills and rent until I started stripping occasionally down at the gentlemen's club. After making at least $600 before the night was over, I picked it up part-time. My mother disapproved of it, but I still did it because it was keeping me and my son straight.

Every guy in the neighborhood tried talking to me, and hell I don't blame them. My thighs and ass fully developed with the help of Jr. because before I got pregnant, I was nothing but bones. Now nobody can crack those skinny girl jokes on me because I'm a thick redbone and loving it. I took me a quick shower then went to sleep after checking on my baby one last time.

Yatta

"Nique, what time you coming back home?"

"Around twelve."

I watched my fiancé, Unique, as she got dressed to head out for the night. Me being the man that I am, believed her when she said she was going to spend time with her girls, and I was willing to give her space. I've been with Unique damn near my whole 23 years of living. Our mothers were best friends, so we were always around each other. When we became teenagers, we made it official. I'm not going to lie and say I didn't love her because nobody on this earth can say or do anything that will come between us.

As I began to tie my dreads up, one of my homeboys called my phone.

"Yo, what's up Jay?"

"Shit man, what you on for the night?"

"Shit, chilling in the crib. What you on?"

"Man not a damn thing, trying to get high."

"A'ight bet, slide through."

"Bet."

When I hung up, I focused my attention back on Unique's sexy, dark skin ass as she began putting a pair of pumps on.

"Hold the fuck on, where y'all going for you to be dressed like that?"

"To a lounge downtown."

"You not going wearing that, so take that shit off and change that whole fuckin' outfit you got on."

She began huffing and throwing the pumps she just had on across the room.

"Aye, what the fuck is your problem, g?"

"What you mean, what's the problem? I can never wear what the fuck I want, it's just a waste buying the shit Yatta!"

"First off, lower your fuckin' tone. Second, you are my fiancé now, so why the fuck would I let you go out dressed like that? And third, you always buy that shit without me knowing because you already know I don't play that shit."

"A'ight, whatever Yatta."

I watched her take the short ass dress off, and change into some distressed jeans and a fancy, teal top that she got from Akira's store. Unique wasn't the thick type, but she wasn't real skinny either; she was just right for me. After putting on some silver sandals, she gave me a kiss then left out the door. I swear she could be a fucking handful sometimes, but that's why I loved her so much. She's the only female I've been in a serious relationship with. After I finished wrapping my dreads up, I heard a knock on the door.

"Who is it?"

"Me, nigga."

I opened the door to let my boy in before heading towards the kitchen. Jay and I played cards while we smoked some weed talking about life. Jay has been my nigga since day one. He and my nigga Chris been around each other since diaper days. They were the only ones I needed in my circle, and of course Unique's ass. The three of us been running the streets, and with our business taking off, money wasn't a problem for any of us.

"Bro, we should go hit up the gentleman's club real quick," Jay said to me as we finished our card game and lit a third blunt.

"You know I'm engaged, I can't be up at no strip club."

"Nigga, so what! You don't know what the hell Unique out there doing with her girls."

"But I trust her."

"She ain't gotta know you went bro, only if you tell her."

I thought for a second, then got up and looked for something to wear. After taking a quick shower, I put on my black, Just Do It shirt by Nike with some black jogging pants to match. Leaving my hair wrapped up in a ponytail to the back, I decided to put on my gold, heart-shaped chain, which had a picture of my mother and my brother side by side. Every time I went somewhere I made sure they were always with me.

Getting ready to head out, I grabbed my keys and sprayed on some Ralph Lauren cologne.

"Aye nigga, you driving. This was yo' idea."

I watched as Jay shook his head and unlocked the doors to his all black, 2015 Bentley Continental GT; I have the same car, but mine is all white. We both got inside and headed to the club. I kissed my chain and began to flame up another blunt.

Since my big brother, Gee, was killed two years ago, my mindset changed. It was like I was following in his footsteps but this time, I was making it my business for Chicago to remember our names. Right after he was killed, me and my boys found out who was responsible. Let's just say that nigga is best friends with Satan now. My brother and I use to run the streets of Chicago together, but since he passed I took over the streets; I became the king, and everyone knew about us. I was surprised that the nigga Greg had the balls to take my brother away from me. Greg was an old school dude that hung with my pops, who's now behind bars, back in the day. It was crazy because Greg was like another father to us, so I didn't understand why he would do some shit like that. I mean, when we broke bread, we made sure everyone ate. But I guess he just had to be greedy, now his ass is rotting in hell. That's why I keep my circle small because of snake shit like that.

Chapter Two

"Khadijah, why would you let me know at the last minute? I have things to do today, and I don't think I will make it back in time to watch him."

"Alright ma."

I ended the call and called up my only big sister, Angel, to see if she could watch Jr. for me for tonight.

"What's up, Dijah?"

"Nothing, are you busy tonight?"

"No, why?"

"I need a babysitter while I go to work tonight."

"You know damn well I don't got shit to do tonight. But on some real shit though Dijah, I don't have a problem watching my nephew, but you need to start looking around for a real job."

"What you mean real job? This job real, I'm making money aren't I?"

"It's how you making it. You think that shit is a career?"

I huffed obnoxiously; I really didn't want to listen to one of her fucking lectures.

"Look, I appreciate you watching him for me tonight. I will be on my way in a minute."

I hung the phone up not wanting to hear what she was going to say next. Hell, I really don't give a damn how people felt about me stripping;

I have to do what I have to do to provide for me and my son. What pisses me off is them telling me I have to find a different job. I get what they are saying, but times are hard. It's not like I haven't been filling out job applications, I just haven't received any responses. So for now, I just have to do what pays the bills until I get my nursing license.

After getting Jr. and his bag ready, I locked up the house. I strapped him in his car seat before heading to the driver's seat, buckling my belt and driving off. My sister didn't stay too far from me, so It only took me 10 minutes getting to her house. When she came out to get Jr. and his bag, she gave me a hard stare which I ignored. I smiled at her and kissed my sleeping son before placing him in her arms, and then I rushed back to the apartment so I could shower and get myself ready. As I got out of my car and walked up the steps to my porch, I noticed Kenny sitting on the top step. He stood up when he saw me approaching. I just rolled my eyes and proceeded to enter my apartment on the first floor.

When I let him inside, he sat at the dining room table and held one of Jr.'s toys he picked it up from the floor in his hands.

"you know, I'm really sorry about the way I acted towards you and Jr. Where is he?"

"At my sister's house."

"You think you could forgive me?"

"No."

He let out a sigh then looked up at me with his dark brown eyes.

"I hear you working at that strip club."

"Yeah."

"Why? You know people still know you are the mother of my child. That shit is embarrassing man."

"Don't come in my fuckin' house trying to tell me what other motherfuckers know, and that you're embarrassed by me shaking my ass to put food on the table, clothes on Jr.'s back, and keep my rent and bills paid!"

"Look, I got you okay?"

"You told me that same shit before Jr. was born. So you expect me to believe it now? You haven't done shit for our son since he's been born. I did everything Kenny, and it makes no fuckin' since that you could just get up and walk these streets without even wanting to spend time with your son."

"Look, I apologize, but it's just that my new chick had me so caught up in her and her three kids, that I haven't had time for my own. If you let me get him this weekend, I promise I will get him everything he needs."

"So you been playing stepdaddy to three kids, but your ass has not seen your son's face the whole year he's been alive! Then you turn around and ask can you keep him for the weekend? That's not how shit works, he doesn't even fuckin' know you."

I felt myself getting ready to explode in a few seconds, so I just put my hands up as I felt my face turn hot. I'm not the type of female to keep a man child away from him because I know how growing up without a father feels, and I don't want Jr. to experience that. In this case, we would have to work on something before I just up and let him keep Jr. over a weekend. The only father figure I had after my dad left was my uncle, but he was killed.

"Look, how about you come here on the weekends and visit him? You know, let him get to know you first before you just take him by his self."

"Okay, that's understandable. I'll be back tomorrow then to see my little man."

"Okay."

As he began walking towards the door, he turned around to look at me while licking his lips.

"Aye, Khadijah?"

"Yeah?"

"You know I still love you, right?"

"Boy please, you don't love me."

"I do. I see how thick yo' ass done got, thick thighs and all, and still got that beautiful ass face and eyes."

I rolled my eyes as I walked up to the door, unlocking it so I could show him his way out.

"Don't worry, daddy will be back baby."

I shoved him out the door, then slammed and locked it. That man was crazy as hell if he thought I was ever getting back with him. Not after he left me to do this shit alone. Then had the nerve to tell me he was with some other bitch's kids, but couldn't come see his own son for a whole year. I would never get back with Kenny's ass, ever. Looking at the time on my iPhone 6, I saw that it was ten o'clock and I would be late. I hurriedly jumped in the shower and put my clothes on, packing my work clothes in my duffle bag along with my perfume and other things I needed before I headed off to my job.

When I arrived I was greeted by my homegirl, Shelly, who I've been cool with since I started working.

"Yo ass late as hell."

"I know, I had to drop my son off at my sister's crib since my mama couldn't watch him."

"Well bitch money calling. Come on, you up next."

I made my way to the locker room and switched into my g string. I placed two blue glitter stars over both of my nipples before I let my straight, black, shoulder-length hair down and sprayed on some Victoria's Secret perfume. I put on my blue pumps then made my way to the stage. A guy with a low fade grabbed my arm causing me to look at him crazy.

"Um, excuse you?"

"Me and my friend want a dance, you bad as fuck."

"Well y'all have to wait, I'm up next on stage."

"Cool."

As the D.J. announced my name, the speakers blasted *Kiss It Better* by Rihanna. I climbed on top of the pole and opened my legs wide as I came down doing a split. I bounced my ass to the music as it switched to *Freak Hoe* by Speaker Knockerz. As soon as I got up and started bouncing my ass, hundreds flooded the stage. I climbed up the pole again, this time making sure my legs were wrapped around, and made my ass clap as I slid down. Sitting on the floor, I put my legs up in the air so they could get a good view of my ass as I started to shake it.

When I got through, I picked up all the money and walked off stage. I bumped into the guy who grabbed me again.

"What's up, you gone give me and my guy a dance or what?"

"Depends on how much y'all got."

He pulled out stacks and it made me smile. To be honest, this was one lucky night.

"Okay, I got y'all. Give me a sec."

"No problem."

I hurried to the back to put my money up in my duffle bag and changed into a black, see-through body suit from Victoria's Secret. I made sure I locked my locker, then headed back out to the club scene. When I got to the table where ol' boy with the money was, I peeped his sexy ass friend. I must've stared too long because the one who stopped me was standing in face, talking, and I hadn't seen him move closer to me. He was decent with a low fade, brown skin, and a handsome face, but that dread head friend of his did something to me.

"You and your friend can follow me."

As I walked to the privet area, I seen him signal for the dread head to come on. When I got to the room the dread head spoke up to his friend.

"Aye, why don't you go find another chick?"

"You done lost yo damn mind, I spotted this one."

I chuckled at the fact he was so serious to see me dance.

"I got a friend for you," I said to the dude with the low fade.

I looked around to find Shelly and she walked to me right on time.

"Aye, Shelly give this man a private dance."

I shot her a wink to let her know he had good money. She smirked at me as she looked at him while his eyes roamed her thick frame.

"I'll see you in a min Yatta."

Me and his dread head friend laughed at how he was walking behind Shelly's ass. When they were out of sight, I walked into the private room and dread head followed, closing the door behind him. I went over to the radio and played Ann Marie's *Make Love* as he took a seat on the sofa. I seductively walked closer towards him, and he wrapped his hands around my waist as I straddled him. I grinded my hips into his pelvis, moving with the beat as my ass popped on top of him. The way his hands felt on my skin had sparks shooting through me. Never have I had this feeling from anyone, so it was kind of awkward for me, but I continued to dance for him.

When the music ended, my body suit was halfway off revealing my nice B-cup breasts. I got off of him and turned away as I fixed my suit. Now that my breasts weren't out, I turned back around and jumped a little because he was directly in front of me.

"What's your name, beautiful?"

"Khadijah, yours?"

"I'm Kenyatta, but I go by Yatta. Can I get your number? You too good to be up in here like this."

"I'm sorry, but I can't give you my number, and right now it's making me money so I don't want to hear any of your lectures, Yatta."

He stepped back, but still looked at me like he had something else he wanted to say.

"Alright. I'll be seeing you around, sweetheart."

He gave me one more stare down then dropped four thick stacks on the sofa and exited the room.

When the door closed, I ran over and picked up the money to see that it was all hundreds. I put it inside my suit with a smile and walked out, ending my night early. Yatta seemed like a nice person, but I was not in need of a relationship. All niggas were problems that I didn't need. It was only about me and my son.

Yatta

The next morning came and Unique's ass still hadn't come back from last night. I've been calling her phone, but there was no answer so I decided to see what my guys were on. Chris wasn't picking up so I called Jay and discussed some business we needed to talk about.

Khadijah's sexy ass was still heavy on my mind and I didn't know why. After my shower, I let my dreads hang down and began to get dressed. I was the type of nigga that had money but didn't really buy all that expensive shit. On occasion I would go all out, but other than that I would just be walking around in regular ass jeans and t-shirts. My shoe game was crazy though. Since winter was coming to an end I still wore my wheat Timbs.

Pulling up to the barbershop I owned out east, I stepped out and walked in. My staff was a group of crazy talented individuals whose ages ranged from 19 to 45; There is a mix of races and even two female barbers. Dapping a few of my staff members, I stopped and talked with them for a while before I finally headed to my office in the back. Sitting down in my chair, I pulled out my key to my lock box and opened it. After I removed a few stacks of money, I started counting.

"Who is it?" I asked after there was a short, but loud knock on my door.

"Jay, man."

"Come in."

My eyes stayed glued on the money, but I saw Jay sit in the chair in front of my desk.

"I'm mad you fucked up my dance with that bitch at the club."

"Watch yo fuckin' mouth."

"Damn, okay bro." He held his hands up in defense with one eyebrow raised then it got quite.

"Damn man, that's all you?" he asked looking at all the money.

"Of course."

"You need to put that shit in the bank or something."

"Yeah, I been thinking that."

"True. So what you wanted to talk about?"

"Are you satisfied with the way your money coming?"

"Yeah, why you ask that?"

"I was thinking we need more guys on the block moving the weight for us, so we can double up on the cash."

I watched as Jay rubbed his chin which told me he was thinking about it.

"I also want to put out a new product out."

"And what's that?"

"Some new pills."

"Aw, okay cool, so when this supposed to be happening?"

"Sooner than you think."

I reached towards my safe, put in the code, and pulled out two bags filled with the new pill product. I watched as a smile spread across Jay's face.

"So when you gone put it on the streets?"

"Shit, maybe by the end of the week if we can get more guys working."

"True, well I got you. I'm gone make sure I have some new, trustworthy, loyal niggas on the block by the weekend."

"Okay, cool. You talked to that nigga Chris today?"

"Naw, I spoke with him last night though. He said him and some chick was going out."

"True."

My mind went back to Unique and her not answering the phone, so I made a note in my head to call her ass again. If they were messing around, I honestly wouldn't hesitate to end both of their asses. My thoughts came to an end after Jay snapped his fingers to get my attention.

"You good, bro?"

"Yeah, I'm straight."

"Well I'm gone get up out of here, I got things to do. I'll see you tomorrow or something."

"Okay."

Jay got up and walked out of the room and I pulled out my phone to call Unique, but again I got the voicemail. Wait 'til I got home, it was going to be one hell of a war. I got up and walked back to the front after putting my money and product back in the safe. My heart literally skipped a beat as my eyes laid on Khadijah again, this time with a little boy with her. I had an open chair since everyone else had customers, so I decided to walk up to her beautiful ass.

"Nice seeing you again, how are you doing today?"

"Fine, just waiting to get my son's haircut."

She looked like she was a bit embarrassed but that didn't bother me.

"Well, my chair is available. I can cut it."

She gave me a look of relief that she didn't have to wait any longer.

"Hey little man, what's your name?"

"Kenny."

By the way he talked I could tell he was about one year old, probably going on two.

"You're getting your hair cut today, little man?"

He nodded his head then stood up as I told him to follow me. I helped him get in the chair and wrapped a cape around him. After cutting his hair, I gave him a small mirror so he could see it. I removed the cape as his mother walked to my station, helping him out of the chair. He grabbed on to her hand and I could tell he was a mama's boy, but it was nothing wrong with that, I was one as well.

"How much is it?"

"Nothing, all I need is your number."

She looked at me with a smirk then looked around to see if anyone heard me. Once she realized no one was paying attention, she turned back to me and smiled, showing off her deep dimples. I smiled in return, I couldn't help myself. She was just so beautiful to me plus thick in the right places with no stomach.

"Let me see your phone," she said, as her voice made love to my ears.

I pulled out my iPhone 6 and Unique's name popped up. I ignored her call then went to my dial pad and handed it to Khadijah. I watched as she put her number in my phone and saved it under Dijah.

"It was nice seeing you again, Yatta."

"And it was nice seeing you as well."

After exchanging smiles and saying goodbye to her son, she left and I began browsing through my phone. Unique's ass had sent me back to back texts with a bunch of bullshit ass excuses, but I didn't bother to reply. I would just wait until I got home later.

Chapter Three

Khadijah

I collected the money I made for the night and headed back over to my sister's house.

"Hey, I'm on my way to pick up Jr."

"It's okay, you can come get him in the morning. It's already late."

"Okay, thanks sis. I will call you when I get up."

"Ok."

I hung up the phone thanking God she let me have a little break. With the way I was working, these night shifts were killing me. It was now two in the morning and I was just making it in the house. After showering and cleaning up a bit, I was too tired to count the money I made tonight so I just sat the duffle bag to the side as I made my way to the bed. I took a look at my phone and saw that Yatta texted me earlier so I made a note to myself to text him back when I woke up. Putting my phone on the charger, I went off into a deep, well needed slumber.

Yatta

"Why the fuck weren't you answering the phone?" I questioned Unique as she sat back in the bed like she ain't have a care in the world.

"I told you I went back to Tasha's and fell asleep. I was drunk, I didn't hear my phone Yatta."

"So you think it's cool yo' ass stayed out all night?"

"No, but what you expect?"

"Fuck you mean, what I expect? For you to bring yo' ass home, or at least fuckin' pick up your damn phone and let me know something!"

"Okay, and I called you back as soon as I got up. Why the fuck you ain't answer? You sent me straight to the voicemail! Not to mention yo' ass scrolling in here at seven in the morning yelling at me."

"I was working, don't fuckin' question me. Yo' ass should have answered when I called the first fuckin' time!"

I watched as she scrolled through her phone blowing her breath. I didn't want to believe Unique was cheating on me, but the way she was acting left me no choice.

"So who you been seeing?"

Her eyes nearly bulged out of her skull as she looked at me.

"Nobody Ya, why you ask me that?"

"No reason."

I got fed up with her so I just walked off into the basement. After I sent Khadijah another text, I waited for a response. While waiting Chris called my phone.

"What up?"

"Nun, I see you been calling me. What's up?"

"I already discussed it with Jay."

"Aw, so you don't need me to do nothing?"

"Not right now, but I'll hit yo' line as soon as something come up," I lied.

"A'ight."

Chris gave me this funny feeling I couldn't explain, something was just off about him. I couldn't put my finger on it now, but from now on I'd just keep business between Jay and I. I hit up Jay and told him not to tell Chris anything. After hanging up the phone, I saw that Dijah responded back saying she had just gotten up so I told her good morning.

"Why you come down here?" Unique had the nerve to ask.

"Why does it matter?"

"Because I thought we were talking."

"I'm done talking to you."

"So what's your problem, Yatta?"

"Nothing."

I watched as Unique walked back upstairs then I began to text Khadijah back.

Unique

When I got out of the shower I noticed Yatta was gone. I really was tired of his shit and wanted so badly to tell him that I was messing with his best friend, Chris. Chris and I have been messing around for almost a year now. I developed strong feelings for him over that year even though I've been knowing him for years because like I said, he was Yatta's friend. I called him up to let him know he could come over because Yatta wasn't here.

I know what I'm doing is wrong, but right now I don't care. I'm young and I don't want to be tied down, but I'll never tell Yatta that because he's my meal ticket. Without him I would probably be homeless somewhere because I have no family to turn to. Right now, I'm just enjoying myself and hoping I won't get caught. And by the look of things, that won't be anytime soon.

When Chris arrived, I began to smile from ear to ear. Being around him made me happy. Not that I wasn't happy with Yatta, but Chris made me feel a different way about him. He's 6'0", the same height as Yatta, and he kind of favors Chris Brown. I laid on the bed and stared at him as he took his clothes off.

I usually don't bring Chris to the house, but I did so today because I felt the tension in the air with Yatta earlier so I knew he wasn't coming home soon. Just as Chris laid between my legs with his thick girth pushing inside of me, my phone started to go off. He lifted up off of me and I picked up my phone, reading a text from Yatta.

"You think you slick?"

My eyes got big, feeling my heart damn near beat out of my chest. I started to become paranoid as if he was watching me.

"Chris, you have to go!"

"Why, what's up?"

Showing Chris the text, he hurried to put his clothes back on and I did the same. I made sure to sneak him out through the back way. Feeling like I was about to faint, I locked the doors then rushed upstairs back to my cell phone which was now ringing.

"Hello?"

"Who the fuck you have in my house?"

Feeling light headed, I licked my dry lips then began to speak.

"Nobody Yatta."

"You sure about that?"

"Yeah, why you asking?"

"Just called to fuck with you, but you do know I have eyes everywhere so don't let me find out yo' ass is lying."

"Ain't nobody lying to you, boy."

I smacked my lips then grabbed my chest, beginning to calm down. I was over here sweating bullets thinking his ass was watching me. My life would have ended in seconds.

"A'ight."

After Yatta hung up, I let out a long sigh. I'm never bringing Chris's ass over here again, now I have to clear some of the tapes he got recording.

Chapter Four

Khadijah

Today was the day that Kenny was supposed to come and see Jr. I've gotten no call or text from him, and it was getting late. Just like always his ass didn't show. I wasn't tripping, now he's completely cut out of my life for good and I mean that. Good thing I didn't get Jr.'s hopes up just to be let down by his no good, deadbeat ass father. I feel so bad that I chose him to be Jr.'s father, but he made everything sound so good and had me thinking we were going to be a family. I guess that's where girls fuck up at, believing that bullshit. But hey, everyone has been dumb over a nigga at least once in their lives. I just wish my baby boy had a real father.

After feeding and bathing Jr., I got him into bed. Once he was tucked in I gave him a kiss on his forehead, turned on his night light, and walked back to my room. Since today was my day off, I decided to have company over so I told Yatta he could come over for a while. I know I said I wasn't looking for a relationship but I do want one, a girl like me needs the extra company. I had already had a bath and washed my hair. Since my mother was white, I inherited her hair texture and my hair naturally curled when wet. I didn't wear anything too reveling because I didn't want to give off the impression that I wanted to fuck on the first night. Someone began knocking on the door, and I was about to run to the door but then caught myself and slowed down. Looking through the peephole I saw it was Kenyatta, so I fixed up a bit then unlocked and opened the door.

I watched as he walked inside then I closed and locked my door.

"You look beautiful."

"It smells beautiful in here too," he said as he looked around my front living room.

I smiled at his polite complement and watched his eyes dance over my body.

"Thank you. You don't look bad yourself and I like your hair."

I sat in awe at how his dreads were freshly designed into zigzags going to the back. I did hair but dreads were my thing, I was always excited to learn new designs.

"Thank you baby, I just have to ask…"

"Ask what?"

"Are you mixed with anything?"

"Yes, my mom is white my dad is black. What made you ask?"

"Your eyes seem to change colors. When I met you they were light grey, at the shop they were a bit darker, and looking at them now they're a light greenish color, and of course your hair. You don't look like the type to wear fake shit so I had to ask."

"Yeah, I don't put any weave in my hair and my eyes changes on their own."

He gave me a smile that I couldn't resist which caused me to smile back.

"So light green must mean you're happy to see me?"

I couldn't help but laugh at him, he was too cute with that comment.

"Yes, I'm happy."

We both laughed. He looked around the living room where we sat on the couch.

"Where is little man?"

"He's asleep."

"Does he spend time with his father? If you don't mind me asking."

I paused for a second, hesitant to answer the question. I didn't want him judging me.

"It's a long story."

He looked down at his watch then back up at me, I guess trying to be funny.

"I got nothing but time, sweetheart. That's what I'm here for, so we can get to know each other."

He gave me a sincere look then I let out a light sigh.

"Well, I met my son's father when I was in my second year of high school. He and I are the same age, I'm twenty-one by the way, so he was everything to me. We did what normal couples do, he was my first and we were careful about sex because we didn't want any kids then. But when I got pregnant, he began to change. He would have females calling his phone, texting, and everything. He would always promise that it was just me and him but I knew that was lie. When I gave birth to my son, he completely disappeared. He later had the nerve to tell me he can't be a father right now because he's still young. My mother paid for me to get this apartment after she put me out. For a while she paid the rent and bills until I could handle it."

"That nigga tweaking, he fucked up sweetheart. For one, you look too damn good, probably better than the females he fuckin' around with. And two, you don't deserve to be raising a child on your own. Especially a young boy. I always wanted a little boy."

I watched as a distant expression crossed his face so I decided to ask him a question.

"Are you in a relationship?"

Right then and there I knew I shouldn't have asked that question because I was not ready for the answer.

"Honestly, yes I am. I'm engaged."

I don't know why, but my heart sunk and my thoughts of being with him were now dead.

"How long you been engaged?"

"About six months now."

I gave him a look as to say, *why are you sitting in my face and why were you at a strip club if you're engaged.*

"Don't look like that though, I'm not a cheater. I just feel different about her these last couple of days. She's been acting strange as hell."

"What you mean?"

"I get this feeling like she's out doing some dirt, but I haven't looked into it how I want to because I'm afraid of what I might do."

If he was referring to killing her then I knew he must be in love with her.

"We've known each other our whole lives. When we were teenagers, we decided we were going to be a couple. From there we been cool, but I'm just now noticing her changes and I believe she's messing around on me. I feel it. We haven't had sex in like two weeks. It's just crazy for me right now."

I felt my heart skip a beat. I don't know why, but I felt his pain. I mean I would be mad as hell, probably pass the limit of pissed off, at the thought of getting cheated on. He seems like a nice guy and he's fine as hell so I don't know who in their right mind would cheat on him.

"You know the saying what's done in the dark will come to light?"

"Yeah."

"Well, whatever she's doing its going to come to light. You own that shop I took my son to?"

"Yeah, my granddad left it to me before he passed a couple years ago. I know you strip but what else you do for a living?"

"I'm not the judging type, so it's cool whatever you do," he said after I didn't respond.

"I'm taking online classes."

"That's cool, what you taking up?"

"I'm studying to become a nurse."

"Okay, you know how to do hair?"

"Yeah, sew ins, braids, dreads, anything you name. I learned from my oldest sister."

"How would you like it if I asked you to stop stripping and work at my cousin's salon? It's right next to my shop and she's been looking for some more beauticians."

"I would love to. I hate stripping anyway. The only reason I do it is because I haven't received any offers from jobs I've applied for, so I had to do what I had to do, you know?"

"I feel you, but I don't want to hear about you up at anyone's club from now on."

"I thank you so much!"

The fact that this man didn't sit here and judge me like others would have had me feeling him, but the thought of him having a fiancé crossed my mind again.

I felt butterflies in my stomach as he got up and walked over to sit next to me.

"You're welcome sweetheart."

We stared at each other for a moment before our lips met and it felt so right, but I pushed back not wanting to go any further with him. I guess he knew because he got up and walked to the door, and I followed him. We hugged, and the way his body felt against mine was a feeling I wanted to last.

"I will be seeing you soon, Dijah."

"Okay, Yatta."

When he walked out, I locked my door and ran to the bathroom to take another shower. The way he had me feeling was a damn mess, had my underwear wet and he ain't even do that much. I could see that I was going to have to behave myself around him like I did today because Lord knows I will snatch his ass up quick. Just the thought of him going back home to his fiancé made me feel some type of way.

Chapter Five

Unique

After getting up from the bed, I felt an awkward feeling come across me and had this extreme urge to throw up. Running to the bathroom, I lifted the toilet seat up and began throwing up. After flushing the toilet and washing my mouth out, I walked back to the bedroom and sat on the bed feeling my head begin to spin. Yatta turned and looked at me causing me to hide my face with my hands.

"What's up with you?"

"I don't know, I don't feel good."

"How long you been doing that?"

"Doing what? "

"Throwing up and shit."

"I really haven't paid any attention, but maybe four weeks and I haven't come on this month."

I watched as he sat up in the bed then began to sigh rubbing his forehead.

"You need to make an appointment."

I looked at him and our eyes met. At that moment I felt so bad for cheating on him. Not to mention I wouldn't know who my child's father was because I had been sleeping with the both of them back to back without using any protection. I nodded my head at his words and picked up my phone to schedule an appointment for next week. I wanted to go before then, but that was the only time my doctor would be available so

I was going to head to the store and buy some home pregnancy tests. I was curious, and scared at the same time to find out if I was pregnant.

"You want to go buy a test?" Yatta asked me as he put some clothes on while I was still stuck sitting in the bed.

"No, I can wait."

"Okay, so that means no drinking or smoking until you find out, and don't be around others that do it."

"Don't start this shit, Yatta."

"What you mean, don't start? You think you pregnant with my seed then that's what the fuck I mean, and don't let me catch your ass under any influence."

"Whatever."

"Yeah I know."

"Where you going?"

"Work."

"You gone be straight?" he asked looking at my now scrunched up face.

"Yeah."

"A'ight, call my phone if you need anything. Don't leave this damn house for nothing."

"Damn, now I can't fuckin' go anywhere!"

"Hell naw, that's why I just said if you need anything to call me."

"You really irritating me right now so just leave."

"Cool. But like I said, don't leave this damn house."

I rolled my eyes at him as he walked out of the room. Shortly after I heard the front door slam and his car starting up. He must have lost his mind telling me to stay in the house like I was a damn child. He should have known I wasn't staying in this house. I got up and did my morning hygiene, made myself something to eat, and then headed out the door.

Khadijah

Today I start my new job as a beautician which has been my dream since I was in high school. After I told my mother, she was all for keeping Jr. for the day, and my sister was happy for me. After getting Jr.'s things together and packing them, I put everything in the car. I put Jr. in his car seat then sat in the front seat as I put on some red lipstick. I gave my curls a few twists then I was on my way to drop Jr. off. Once I dropped him off to my mom's, I was headed to work.

I had already met Yatta's cousin, the owner, and she was cool as hell. She's a dark-skinned, slim thick female with a beautiful face. I felt comfortable around her. She's eight years older than me though, but I didn't care; We had a lot in common. When I pulled up to the salon, I saw Yatta standing outside of his shop talking on his phone. His call ended as he watched me approach.

I knew I had his attention because of my attire. I had on a fancy, blue stripped shirt that cut off above my flat belly, showing off my piercing, and jeans that showcased my curves and ass. When I got closer to him he started licking his lips and I smiled.

"Hey, Yatta."

I waved at him as I attempted to walk pass, but he grabbed my arm lightly, pulling me close to him while pushing his dreads out of his face.

"You looking beautiful today."

"Thank you. And I appreciate you getting me in the salon."

"That's all you," he said. "You want to go get lunch on your break?"

"Yeah, sure."

"Cool, just text me before you go on break, sweetheart."

"Okay."

As I turned around to walk into the salon, I felt Yatta's eyes glued on my back side. I couldn't help but smile as I walked into the salon. I saw Yatta's cousin, Keshia getting her seat and booth ready while another chick did the same while looking at me.

"Heyyy Dijah girl!"

"Hey Keshia, how are you?"

"I'm fine, how about yourself?"

"I'm okay."

"That's good. This is Tonya, Tonya this is our newest beautician, Khadijah."

I reached my hand out and she did the same, looking like she wanted to say something.

"Okay Dijah, it was only two of us but we got the job done, so now that it's three, business should start to become easier. I already seen most of your work, do you have any personal clients coming in?"

"Yeah."

"Okay, good."

I began setting up my area, which was across from Tonya's. The name sounded familiar to me, but her face didn't match the person I thought about. I didn't have a clue why she kept staring at me but it was starting to work my nerves. An hour went pass and I had already did my first customer's head. Down at the strip club, I let all the females know to come down and get their hair done. That was a quick $250. Once I finished, I sat in my chair as Keshia and Tonya worked on their clients while I waited for the next customer to come in. I took the free time to call my mother to check up on Jr., and shortly after it was lunch time.

After coming back from the bathroom I saw Yatta's ass standing next to his cousin as she was doing her finishing touches on her client's sew in. Tonya had already finished and was walking in my direction. She stopped once she got in front of me.

"So you don't remember me, chick?"

My eyebrows furred together in confusion.

"Excuse me?"

"You heard me, so you don't recognize who I am yet?"

I thought long and hard because I couldn't recall meeting her anywhere. I guess I took too long because she smacked her lips then put her hands on her hips.

"We went to Bouchet together."

"Oh my God! Tonya how are you!"

She smiled then held her arms out so we could hug and I did just that. She looked so different from elementary school. Me and her were tight as super glue through first to eighth grade. That was my right hand, but then we lost contact. We linked back up around the time I was messing with Kenny then lost touch again. She looked great; she was a little thick, but her arms were skinny and she still has that rich, chocolate skin with those big, pretty eyes of hers. The reason I didn't recognize her was because she was wearing too much make up and she was too pretty for that.

"I've been good, I've been staying down the street from the salon for like two years now. How you been, Ms. light bright?"

"I've been good. I live a couple of blocks away myself."

"That's good. Well give me your number so we can talk more. You want to go to lunch and catch up?"

I looked over to Yatta who was now staring at me. Tonya caught on and threw her hands in the air playfully with her phone in her hands.

"Well okay, I see you."

We both laughed then exchanged numbers and she went on her break. I walked over to Yatta and his cousin.

"You ready, Dijah?"

"Yeah, which restaurant we going to?"

"Whichever one you want, it's on me."

"Mhm, y'all need to stop playing around and get together," Keshia interjected.

Yatta shot his cousin a glare that only she could read.

"What, nigga? All I'm saying is y'all need to give it a try. That no good, sneaky bitch you with is going to cause trouble in your life. Believe me, I read people very well. Besides, you need someone new."

Laughing at Keshia I shook my head.

"You a mess, Keshia."

"I'm just saying."

"Stay out my business, cuz."

"Okay. Remember Dijah, you get an hour break."

"Okay."

Yatta and I walked out then headed to Fred and Jack's which wasn't that far from the salon. It wasn't a lot of people inside so we were in and out with our food. We sat in Yatta's car and ate. Once we were done I began to start up a conversation with him, but someone else had his attention. Before I knew it, he was getting out of the car walking over to some dark chocolate, skinny chick, but she was beautiful. I opened the door and stood by it while I watched Yatta.

"Unique, why the fuck are you out the house!"

I heard him from where I was standing because he was loud as fuck. I could see the girl's lips moving, but couldn't hear anything. However, I could tell by the way she was moving her hands and rolling her neck that she was giving him a smart response back. A few minutes later, he threw his hands up in the air and walked off on her with her screaming his name. He just ignored her, but she followed right behind him.

"Get in the car, Dijah."

By the time I opened the door, she was in front of him yelling, pointing her finger in my direction.

"Oh, so this why you wanted me to stay in the house? So you can parade this fake ass bitch around!"

"Excuse you, I don't know you and you don't know me, so keep that bitch word to yourself."

"Bitch shut the fuck up! I'm talking to my man, this ain't got shit to do with you. Stay yo' fake ass over there! Matter of fact close that door bitch because you not getting in that car."

"Make me close it then, bitch!"

Punk was not in my bloodstream. I didn't care who it was, no female was about to talk to me or treat me like I was some type of clown because these hands would send a bitch to a straight into a coma. When she was about to come around to my side, Yatta grabbed her by her waist.

"Aye, chill the fuck out man. Take yo' ass back to where ever the fuck you were goin'."

"So this how you treat me, Yatta? You fucking that fake, weave wearing, light bright, contact wearing ass injected hoe?"

When she said that, I promise you I wanted to knock that bitch the fuck out. Everyone was now looking in our direction. Hell, a few cars stopped to look, but what she said didn't faze me because little did she know, ain't shit about me fake. This is all natural over here, but she ain't nobody to explain shit to.

"All that is unnecessary, Nique. Just take yo' ass on. I will deal with you later!"

"A'ight, that's cool."

I watched as she walked off then Yatta turned to me with apologetic eyes. I got back in the car without saying a word to him. I guess he could tell I was mad because when we pulled back up to the shop, he turned to me and grabbed my hand before I could get out.

"Look, I apologize for that back there. That was my fiancé."

"Yeah, I figured. It's okay though."

"Okay. Can I see you tonight?"

"Um after that back there, I think you should go home to your fiancé."

Yatta let out a long sigh before turning back to look at me.

"So I can't talk to you no more?"

"Not with how your fiancé acting, and we not even fucking. I don't want her to think nothing like that because I'm a female before anything, and I don't want to come in between y'all."

"So what you saying?"

"I'm saying I don't want to be your side chick, Yatta. You have a fiancé, and I would've been upset too if I saw you getting in a car with another female."

"Okay Khadijah, I can't do nothing but respect that."

"I mean, we can still be cool, but as far as you coming to spend time with me? I don't think we should do that."

"That's fine. I'll talk to you later."

I gave Yatta a once over, he was so sexy to me. He pushed his dreads that were hanging to the back, showing his smooth, caramel skin and handsome face. Taking the keys out the car I could tell he was mad, but we went our separate ways and carried on with our day.

Chapter Six

Yatta

Walking into my bedroom I could hear Unique's ass whispering on the phone, but when I opened the door she quickly hung up the phone, staring at me with an attitude.

"So you had fun with that bitch today?"

"I'm not in the fuckin' mood, Unique."

Stripping down to my boxers, I laid in the bed and turned my back towards her.

"Well, while you were out being a hoe, I took a few pregnancy tests and they all came back positive."

I turned around and sat up facing her with excitement in my eyes.

"But I don't think it's a good idea to keep it because you and I are not ready for a child right now. I mean, look at today, you out driving a bitch around like y'all together and shit."

"Watch your fuckin' mouth first of all, and second of all, yo' ass not getting an abortion so you can get that wicked shit out of your mind right now."

"Why would I bring this baby into this fucked up situation?"

"What the fuck you mean, fucked up situation?"

"I mean, why would I bring a child into this world knowing its parents are going downhill."

"And how you figure that? You're my fiancé, right?"

"Oh now I'm your fiancé, but just earlier you were treating me like shit to impress that bitch you was with."

"Again, watch your mouth. She works at Keshia's salon. I just took her to lunch, that's all. She knows you're my fiancé."

"She knows, but that ain't stop her from getting in the car."

"She's not that type."

"You defending her now? Okay."

"Look, I'm not defending nobody. I'm just saying you don't have anything to worry about. You're going to stress our baby so cut the shit out, you know nobody's going to take your spot."

"Okay."

"Now give me some loving."

I laid back in the bed as Unique climbed on top of me. After pulling my boxers off, she took all of me in her mouth. One thing about unique was she gave some nice ass head and the thought of her giving it to someone else drove me over the edge. When I pulled her arm so she could climb on top, I slid right into her. With her bouncing up and down I decided to take matters into my own hands and pulled her closer to me while I held on to her. I began fucking her with quick, deep strokes causing her to scream out. I switched positions as I got on top and held her legs back onto the headboard. I began to pound inside her roughly as her nails scratched me up. I then decided to lay my head in the crock of her neck and slow down. After a few more pumps, we both climaxed and I got off of her and went to the bathroom to take a quick shower. The entire time in the shower I thought about Khadijah. I felt different about her, I needed her. I wanted her, but with Unique having my baby, I had to figure out a way to work things out.

Khadijah

After working at the salon for a month, I was making good money. Jr. was off at my sister's house for a sleepover with her kids, so I took the free time to apply for more jobs. Feeling satisfied with filling out four applications, I laid back in my bed just as my phone started to ring.

"Hello?"

"Hey sweetheart, how you and little man been?"

I smiled a little at hearing Yatta's voice. Since the day his fiancé acted belligerent, we haven't spoken at all.

"We are fine. How are you?"

"I'm straight. When can I come see you?"

"What you mean?"

"When can I come over?"

"I don't think it's a good idea."

"Why? I haven't seen or spoken to you in over a month."

"That's not my problem, you haven't been at the shop."

"I been handling other business."

"Oh okay, so how's your fiancé doing?"

I heard him blow his breath in the phone.

"She straight. Why you being like that?"

"Because I'm not with you and the games you trying to run."

"I'm not running no game, I can't come visit you and talk?"

I thought long and hard before I finally gave in.

"Okay, but not that long."

"A'ight."

It was two in the afternoon and here I was in bed looking a mess. My hair was in a messy ponytail, my shirt was extra big, and I had on some fitted jogging pants. I didn't feel like changing so I continued to lay in bed until I heard a knock at the door. Getting up I checked the peep hole and seen Yatta standing on the other side, waiting for me to open up the door.

"Damn, you having a bad day?"

"Naw, just tired."

I watched as he sat on my couch and stared at me as I looked at him.

"She must think you out playing ball or some shit."

I got pissed that he came over dressed in some Jordan shorts with a white t-shirt on and his dreads braided back. Although he was looking fine with his caramel skin complexion and brown eyes, I just couldn't stop myself from catching an attitude.

"I am going to play ball, I just wanted to see you first."

"Why?"

"Because I missed you, that's why."

"I didn't know you could miss another woman other than family and your fiancé."

"What's up with you and this fiancé shit?"

"Because you think I'm a fool. You can't talk to me unless you're a single man."

"So what happened to us being cool?"

"I can't be cool with you."

"Look, I know you feel some type of way because we both feeling each other and I got a fiancée and shit, but real talk, that's not gone stop me from being friends with you and kicking it. So you need to get rid of that attitude shit."

"If I can't have you to myself I don't want to associate with you."

"So you want me to leave my fiancé in order for us to just kick it? That's what you saying?"

"That's exactly what I'm saying."

"A'ight Dijah."

"A'ight what?"

I watched him as he stood up and walked his tall ass over to me. Bending down, he kissed me on my lips causing me to pull back.

"It's not a joke, Yatta, I'm for real. One thing I'm not gone do is fuck with you while you still engaged."

"Why you being so difficult, sweetheart?"

"If it was reversed, you wouldn't fuck with me."

"I personally wouldn't give a fuck."

"Well I give a fuck, and I'm not one of the many thots you be fuckin'."

"I understand that shit."

"I'm not even gone stunt, I feel some type of way about you that's why I'm tripping like this, but I will get over it."

"I feel the same way, but you have to understand that I'm not going to treat you any type of way because of my situation. This past month I couldn't get you out of my head, real shit. Like I can see you in her position."

"You don't mean that last part."

"I do Dijah, it's like I feel a way for you that I can't explain."

"Yeah right."

In a matter of seconds, we ended up French kissing. He picked me up and found his way into my bedroom before he softly laid me on the bed. Taking my clothes off, he kissed my body all the way down to my womanhood. I felt my body shaking as he planted soft kisses on my second set of lips. He began eating me like he hadn't ate in years, causing me to climax twice. Feeling satisfied, he began taking his clothes off and revealing his ten-inch dick which left me speechless. Besides me playing with my toy every night, I haven't had sex for six months.

"Wait, Yatta I'm not on birth control."

"So?"

"Um so, that means you need a condom."

"Baby, I'm straight. I don't have anything and if you get pregnant, so what."

Before I could say anything else, he began kissing me then moved down to my neck.

Feeling his soft lips on my neck interrupted my protest and he used the distraction to his advantage, putting his manhood inside my wet cave. After taking almost all of his ten inches, a tear fell from my eye and he began to rock slow as I had the best orgasm of my life. Speeding up the pace he began to go deep. He was hitting my spot, causing me to moan out in pleasure and him to moan as well. As I came for the second time, he released after me.

He kissed me deeply before laying his head on my stomach. He gave it light, gentle kisses before he got up and walked into my connecting bathroom.

"Where are the wash cloths?"

"On the top rack to the left."

After hearing the water running, he returned and began putting his clothes on.

"What's wrong?"

"I just told you I'm not on birth control."

"Well that's cool, at least I know our baby gone be beautiful."

"Here you go thinking this shit is a joke."

"What you mean? I'm serious."

"I'm not about to be a part of your love triangle."

"Sweetheart, if you get pregnant with my child, I promise you I'm never gonna leave your side."

"That's what my son's father said."

"I'm nothing like that nigga. Between me and you, my fiancé is two months pregnant. But I don't feel any connection, it don't feel like it's mine."

"Do you hear yourself? It's a chance I could be pregnant, but your fiancé already pregnant and you saying you think it's not yours!"

"Hell yeah, I feel that way."

"Look, this too much right now, and this is exactly what the fuck I was talking about."

"I promise you, sweetheart, that I will be here for you always. No matter what."

"So what am I, Yatta?"

"What you mean?"

"What am I to you?"

"My best friend."

"That's all I am to you?"

"Naw, I want you to be more, but I'm trying to see what's up with Unique first."

"So you want me to wait on you?"

"Something like that."

"You got some fuckin' nerve, Yatta. Just get out!"

Without a word being said, he got up and walked out. I then heard my front door slam. Feeling out of place, I began to cry. The decisions I made always fucked me up at the end. Maybe I will just keep my distance from him.

Chapter Seven

Unique

Getting up from Chris's bed, I decided to turn my phone back on. As soon as I did, a swarm of notifications came in. I had twenty-two missed calls and thirty-four text messages from Yatta, basically trying to see where I'm at, and cursing me out for not responding back to him.

"Baby, put that phone up and come lay back down with me so I can rub your stomach."

"Chris, you know that this baby might not be yours?"

"That's my seed, just know I know."

"How you know?"

"Because I get the crazy ass symptoms."

My chest began to go up and down in panic as the thought crossed my mind that this really wasn't Yatta's baby. Maybe I could fake a miscarriage, that way he would never know that Chris was my baby's father. Man I feel bad about treating Yatta this way, but things between him and I have gotten boring. I mean, who's to say he wasn't not out messing around with that chick I seen him with. A part of me wants to purposely hurt Kenyatta because he's just too perfect for me.

That was all going to change once I helped Chris to come up and finesse Yatta's ass. He's been keeping Chris out of the deals that he and Jay have been making, but I had plans on getting that money back to him.

"What kind of symptoms?"

"Throwing up, weird food cravings, and tired as fuck every day."

I thought to myself how our baby would look. I knew it would be beautiful. I've gotten myself in a bad situation that's not going to turn out good, but I need to keep Yatta around and keep that bitch away from him. I grabbed my phone and went to Yatta's Facebook page. I viewed his recently added friends list and there that bitch was. I began stalking her Facebook page trying to find some type of information on her, but paused when I saw Chris was friends with her too.

"How the fuck you know her?"

I shoved the phone in his face so he could get a good look at her profile.

"That's my brother baby mama."

All this time I been knowing Chris, I forgot he had a brother around the same age as him. They have different fathers but I met him a few times. I knew he had a son, but never did he show any pictures of his child's mother. A grin plastered my face as I began looking to find more information on her.

Khadijah

"Hey, little man, how are you?"

"I'm fine."

"Dijah, girl, he looks just like you."

"I wish, he looks like his father to me."

"Well I'm looking at him now and I see you in him."

"I guess."

It was close up time at the salon and my sister had to drop Jr. off to me because she had some where important to go. Looking at my clock it was now 9:30 p.m. I was finishing my customer's sew in as Tonya kept an eye on Jr. for me because she was already done. After finishing up, I swept my area then made sure my table was clean before closing. Jr. held my hand as we walked to the parking lot with Tonya. Reaching my car, I opened it and put Jr. in his car seat then began going to the front door. I waved bye to Tonya as she drove off, and I pulled off after her.

After the fifteen-minute drive, I parked my car and got out. Jr. had fallen asleep, so I had to carry him in my arms. Once I closed my doors and made sure my car was locked I proceeded to walk up the porch steps. Turning into my hallway, there sat Yatta with his head down. After seeing me walk pass him, he stood and began to follow me inside, shutting and locking my front door. As I stepped into Jr.'s room I kept his light off because the new night light I bought him turned on automatically when it got dark. I took off his Jordan shoes, then took his jacket off, and changed him into his night clothes. All that work and he was still knocked out.

Laying him back on his pillow, I kissed his forehead and tucked him in, and a slight smile popped across his face. I turned around and lightly closed his door shut then walked to my bedroom where Yatta was sitting on my bed.

"What do you want? You starting to look like a creep."

"Damn, I can't get a 'hi, how you doing'?"

I folded both of my arms across my chest staring at him with a non-joking expression on my face.

"Okay, I came by to ask you a question."

"A question? You could have called or texted me, Yatta. I'm tired."

"I understand that, I won't be long. I just want to know who is Jr.'s father."

I scrunched my face. Why the hell did he want to know who my child's father is all of a sudden.

"Why?"

"Because now that I think about it, little man looks familiar. I think I know his father."

"His name is Kenny."

I continued to stare at him as he gathered the name into his thoughts then turned to look up at me.

"That's my homie's brother."

"Who's your homie?"

"Chris."

"Aw I didn't know you and Chris were cool, how long y'all been cool?"

"Since we were little kids."

"True, that's what's up."

"Yeah, but yo' baby daddy a hoe."

"That's not nothing new to me. I been found that out."

"I just can't believe a woman like you, so beautiful and sweet, fell into that fuck nigga trap."

"Me either, I was young and dumb thinking he loved me."

I began taking my jewelry off and put it on the night stand. I then took my heels off and sat on the bed next to Yatta.

"Little man looks just like his pops. I was flipping through your Facebook pictures and seen some of his and I just had to ask just to make sure."

"Aww, you all on my Facebook, you miss me?"

"I'm not even about to go there with you."

"Well, you can tell Chris he can check on his nephew every now and then. My baby hasn't even really met his daddy's side of the family and that's sad."

"Yeah, it's sad, but I don't mess with that nigga like that no more."

"Why?"

"He act suspicious that's all, you know you can't really trust too many."

"Yeah, I know that's right. But what is he doing for his behavior to come off as suspicious?"

"Money wise I think he was low key taking a cut on the side. He just gives off this sneaky ass and I'm not feeling it."

"Yeah, you always know your gut feeling. Just watch your back around him."

"Been doing it."

"So how are things going with you and the wife?"

"She's not my wife yet, and it's decent. Her ass been acting suspicious, too. She comes in late and her ass is rarely at home. I gotta crack down on her ass and see what's up."

"So what is it that you think she's doing while she's pregnant with your child?"

"I don't know, you're a female, you tell me."

"Well sounds like her and I are completely different, but from what I'm hearing I would guess she's cheating."

"I knew it. I just wanted to hear it from a female's point of view."

"So what you gone do?"

"She lucky she's pregnant with my baby, or I would kill her and him."

"You shouldn't go that route, just stop fucking with her and co-parent."

"If I find out that shit is true it's going to fuck me up inside."

"Yeah, I know the feeling well."

He turned, looked at me, and lifted my chin with his finger so we were having direct eye contact.

"I couldn't imagine hurting you in any type of way."

"And I couldn't imagine hurting you in any type of way."

We looked at each other for a minute than our lips came together and danced. I couldn't help myself, one minute I was mad at him and the next his ass had me in my feelings.

Chris

Soon as Unique's ass left me I was calling up my main. Tonya is a chick I've been messing around with for two years now. Her and I got this chemistry that me and Unique don't have. Right now I'm just using Unique's ass to get my money back up the way I want then me and Tonya will be gone. I met Tonya through my bro, Kenny. Since Khadijah and her always hung out, I wanted to see what was up with her. We got back in touch through Facebook.

I could see myself marrying Tonya because of her loyalty. I know for a fact she wouldn't fuck me over. Unique on the other hand is pregnant with my seed and we are keeping that a secret until I get this money right. Once I do, me and Tonya leaving Chicago and the bullshit that's in it behind us. Not that I don't care about my baby, but it's all about keeping the love of my life out my side business. I know the shit might sound bad, but when my son or daughter gets older they can find me. I know messing over Yatta is fucked up on my end, but hey, niggas gotta do what they gotta do to survive. Shit, I wanna eat good just like he eating, but even more.

Yet, I kept my plans to myself. I knew them niggas weren't dumb at all, that's why they've been cutting me out of their deals lately. Little did they know, I would be getting that money back soon. A knock on the door got me out of my thoughts and I jumped to answer it. Opening the door, I came face to face with Tonya. She made her way inside as I closed the door. Tonya was different from the rest, her personality was very rare and that was something I admired about her.

Tonya was always to herself; she wasn't out here looking for attention, acting all ratchet like majority of these females were. She knew what she wanted and stuck with that. She got pregnant with my seed a year ago then but the baby was stillborn. We still have our talks about it, but not that much because I know she would get in her feelings quick and be depressed for a whole week. The baby gave her a little meat, so she was thick and just how I liked it: flat stomach, cute face, and ass that you could sit a dinner on.

"Hey baby, how was your day? And why didn't you use the key?"

"Fine. And I didn't feel like digging around in this purse, how was yours?"

I thought about me messing around with Unique all day and hated that I had to lie to her, but it was for the best.

"You know, same old shit."

"How you feel?"

"I'm straight baby, what 'bout yourself?"

"I'm okay. just tired."

"I bought you some chicken, it's in the oven if you're hungry."

"Thank you baby, but all I want right now is you," Tonya said while walking over to me.

I braced myself as Tonya pushed me back on the bed and began to take my shorts down. I got up and pushed her on the bed taking her sundress and underwear off. Like a cat thirsty for milk, my tongue found its way to her moist cave and I began licking away. Hearing her moan got me hard as a rock. Feeling how wet she was with my fingers, I felt satisfied and began ramming into her causing her to scream out in pleasure as she had a smile on her face. That's what I liked about Tonya; she loved when I handled her rough in the bedroom, she's the definition of a lady in the streets and freak in the sheets.

Chapter Eight

Kenyatta

"Yo, you can have this crib. I will make sure everything is paid, but I'm leaving."

"Leaving to go where?"

"I got a spot, don't worry about it."

"Oh, you going to go move in with that chick and her son?"

"First off, I don't have to move in with no female. You know that for a fact so don't do that, and second, how you know she got a son?"

"Because…"

I looked at Unique as she stared at the floor, hesitant to answer the question I just asked her.

"I'm up here."

"My girls talk, and one of them know of her."

"You lying. What you lying for?"

"I'm not lying."

"You starting to piss me off with how you been acting lately. That's one of the main reasons why I'm leaving."

"What the fuck you mean, Yatta!"

"Like the fuck I just said! You starting to piss me off with how you acting, what you hiding man?"

"How you figure I'm hiding something?"

"You never here, you be laughing and shit on your phone, but then when I come in you hang up. Matter of fact, run that phone."

"Fuck you want to go through my phone for? I ain't ask for your shit."

"Give me the shit now!"

I watched her pull the iPhone 6 Plus out of her back pocket then tried to unlock, but I snatched the shit and put in the code. I knew the code because it was the day that we became official. Scrolling through her text messages I side-eyed her as she walked over to the bed and sat down with her head down. I continued to scroll until I seen a message with a contact that had the red kiss lipstick and kiss face emoji on it.

When I clicked on it I saw red as I read messages back and forth saying how much they missed each other, discussing shit about the baby, and how he bought this and that for it.

"Bitch, so the baby not mine!"

Before I could give her a chance to answer, I walked over to her grabbing her arms as tight as I could and lifted her up so we were eye to eye.

"Yatta, let me go, you're hurting me!"

"Answer my fucking question, is the fuckin' baby mine? Who the fuck else you been fucking?"

"I don't know if it's yours. Yatta! I don't know!"

I was only the age of seven when my father killed my mother. Before she passed, she taught me to never put my hands on a woman,

58

no matter how upset I was. Honestly, seeing my own mother get beat to death by my father, that shit changed me a lot. Yet, the fire in me wanted to do the same to this bitch in front of me, but I let her arms go before I blacked out and hurt her.

"Get the fuck out my house, now!"

"Where am I supposed to go, Yatta?"

Her voice was cracking as she cried, looking up at me from the floor.

"Go to your child's father house. Anywhere but here, and give me my fucking ring! This shit over!"

"No, baby, please don't do this! Please I need you, you are all I have!"

"I don't give a fuck what you talking about, Unique, get the fuck out! Matter of fact, keep the fucking ring and keep this shit too."

I took my engagement ring off and threw it at her side. She became horrible to look at as I glared at her with a look of disgust. I couldn't believe she would do this shit to me. I mean I felt something was off about her, but I didn't want to believe it. I at least wanted the baby to be mine.

She got up, grabbed a suitcase, and began filling it with her clothes. I could've been petty and told her ass don't touch none of those clothes because I bought them, but I let it ride. Her ass had everything; she didn't have to worry about shit, but now she had to worry because she ain't got shit to her name. She didn't work, so she had no money saved up. All she did was spend up my money.

"Hurry the fuck up man!"

"Yatta, please I have nowhere to go!"

"You mean to tell me the nigga you fuckin' don't have a place for you? Or you can't go live with him, but you cheated on me for him and he don't have shit! You a sorry bitch! Get the fuck out, man. I'm tired of looking at yo' ass!"

By the time I said that, she had snot running down her noise mixed with the tears that kept rolling down her face. She zipped the suitcase and I began to shove her out the door to the hallway.

"What about my phone! How can I contact anyone?"

"You ain't contacting nobody off my phone, I pay the fucking phone bill. Yo' ass not getting that phone back, go ask yo' baby daddy to buy you another one."

I guess she owned up to her mistakes because she picked her suitcase up, walked down the stairs and out the door which I made sure I locked behind her. I watched as she walked down the block with the big ass suitcase rolling behind her. A part of me still wanted her to stay here and I just go, but fuck that bitch. I don't know who the fuck she thought she was playing.

Khadijah

"Mommy, I want some milk."

Jr. was holding his cup up at me while I got up out of the bed. I couldn't understand why the fuck I felt so tired when I went to sleep at a decent hour last night. I grabbed the cup from him and went to the kitchen as he followed behind me rubbing his eyes. It was only seven-thirty in the morning so I knew he was still sleepy because this was his daily routine. After I filled his toddler cup with milk, I screwed the top back on, put the milk back into the refrigerator and picked him up. I walked back to my room and laid him next to me as I cut the TV on and turned to the Sprout channel. As I rubbed his hair, I checked my phone in the other hand.

Before I could text Tonya back, Yatta's name popped up and I pressed the green button.

"Hello?"

'Hey Dijah, how are you?"

"I'm fine, just tired."

"Can I come see you?"

"What time you trying to do that? I was trying to get some more rest."

"In another hour."

"Okay, well call me when you're outside."

"Okay."

When I hung up, I looked down to at my son. He had fallen back to sleep, so I put my phone down and followed behind him. Two hours later I was up putting Jr. in the tub and getting him dressed for the day. Since today was my off day, I was going to take him to IHOP. When I finished getting him ready, I hopped in the shower as he watched TV. I got dressed in my teal Nike jumpsuit and left my wet, curly hair down. As I put on my Jordan's my phone rung.

"Yeah, Yatta?"

"I'm outside."

I walked to the door with Jr. following me. I let Yatta in and locked my door.

"Hey little man, what's going on?"

Jr. shook his head and Yatta reached his arms out. Jr. went running to him as he picked him up.

"Where y'all going?"

"Out to go eat breakfast."

"Aww, I'm not invited?"

"You can come."

"You missed me?"

He put Jr. down than stepped closer to me as Jr. ran to his room.

"Yeah, I've missed you."

We were so close that his nose and mine were touching. Then our lips met and we kissed for a minute.

"What's up with you, why you acting like that?"

"Acting like what? I missed you, Dijah."

"Okay, Yatta. Come on Jr.!"

Jr. came running as I grabbed my purse and keys, and we were out. Yatta wanted to drive so I put Jr. in his backseat and strapped him down then sat in the passenger seat as Yatta climbed in the driver's seat, pushing his dreads out of his face and began driving.

Our breakfast was great, but it didn't stop there. Yatta came back over to my place and we watched a few family movies. I cooked diner for us, and afterwards we played until Jr. drifted off to sleep. I loved how Yatta interacted with him, it seemed like Jr. and he were starting to have a bond and I loved it. After we laid Jr. in his bed, we walked back to my room.

"You about to leave?"

"No."

"What you mean, no? Yo' fia—"

Before I could get the word out, he put his index finger to my lips and shushed me.

"I don't have one."

I looked at him confused as he showed me his bare ring finger, not that I ever paid attention to it whenever we were together.

"What happened, Ya?"

"Long story short, shorty's ass was cheating the whole time. I found messages in her phone from some other dude talking about the baby, it's not mine."

I could hear how angry he was, but I could also hear his disappointment. I moved his dreads out of his face and pushed him back onto my bed. I closed my door then took my clothes off and he did the same. I climbed on top of him and played with his manhood against my wet cave as he sucked on my nipples, making me release soft moans before putting himself inside of me.

As he continued planting kisses on my neck and sucking on it, I was sure he would leave hickeys, but I didn't care. I continued to ride him nice and slow. He flipped me over gently and began going in and out of me in slow motion. I guess this was what making love felt like because I had a different feeling come over me than ever before. My body felt connected to his as he whispered in my ear.

"I love you, Khadijah."

Him saying that while slow stroking inside of me sent me so far over the edge that I came all over him and the bed.

"I love you too, Yatta."

We kissed with so much passion that I felt him explode in me. Pulling out of me, he rolled next to me and hugged me from behind.

"You probably don't believe me, but I really do love you, Dijah."

"I do, because I love you too, Yatta."

Right then and there I knew God brought him in my life for a reason. He was my soul mate that I had been searching for, and I felt so loved and safe in his arms as he wrapped them tight around me while pulling the covers over us. I reminded myself to get up and change these sheets in the morning. My eyelids became heavy and after hearing Yatta's light snores, I instantly fell asleep.

Unique

I walked through the dark streets of the city and reached Chris's house, but when I knocked and rung the doorbell, he cut his light on then off, and ignored me. After an hour and a half of trying, he came down and told me I couldn't stay there. He didn't even give me any money to get a room or a cab. Luckily, my girl, Tasha stayed four blocks over from Chris, so I went to her spot.

"Girl, what the hell are you going to do? You pregnant and don't have money to support the child, and yo' nothing ass baby daddy using you."

"He's not using me. When I figure out a plan to get back on Yatta's good side, I can hit his ass up and Chris and I are gone move the fuck out of Chicago with our baby."

"Aww, that's what he told you?"

"Yeah."

"If you believe that bullshit, you just as dumb as rocks going up a hill. Bitch he won't even let you stay with him, why is that?"

"Because bitch that's fuckin' up the plan. If motherfuckers see me coming in and out of Chris's place, word gone spread and our plan gone be blown."

"Whatever, Unique. I'm just trying to talk some since into your ass. You sure you want to keep this baby?"

"Yes, I do."

"Well words from your bitch, you done fucked up."

"I haven't. Yatta's just upset right now, he can't stay mad forever. Not at me."

"Bitch, please, that man ain't thinking about yo' lying, cheating ass. Especially now that he knows the baby ain't his."

"When the baby's born, I'll get a DNA test so that will solve everything."

"Why you just won't do the one where they perform the test while pregnant?"

"Bitch, that cost hell of money."

"So ask Yatta to pay for it."

I thought to myself, if I could get Yatta to pay for the test to be done, I could get on his good side in the meantime.

"Let me see your phone, T."

When Tasha handed me her phone, I began to call Yatta's number.

"Hello?"

"Hey, Yatta."

I heard him sigh over the phone.

"Man, what the fuck you want, Unique? I'm busy."

"I want to get the DNA test done."

"Don't you have to wait 'til the baby is born?"

"No, it's one where you could have it done while you're still pregnant. They have a way of going inside your uterus to do it."

"Okay, get it done then."

"I don't have the money, it's 800 dollars."

"I'll see what I can do, but if it comes back negative, you or that nigga better pay my fuckin' money back."

Before I could respond, he hung up and Tasha just stood there looking scared for me. I just laid back onto the couch staring up at the ceiling with my hand on my two-month pregnant belly.

Chapter Nine

Chris

When Unique's ass showed up at my crib at one in the morning, I was thankful my baby Tonya wasn't here. She was spending time with her mother because she became sick, so she was taking care of her until a home nurse showed up. Opening my weed bag I pinched out enough to make me a blunt and still have enough to sell. Since Yatta's ass didn't want me in on shit he's doing, I had to hit up some young niggas around the area and they put me on with this Kush to sell, so it was something in my pocket.

Right when I took a puff of my blunt, my phone started to ring.

"What's up, Jay? My nigga what you been on?"

"Shit, chilling. What yo' ass been on?"

"Shit, dry as hell. When Yatta ass gone put me back on?"

"I don't know, you gotta talk to him about that shit. I was calling to see if you going to this club downtown, tonight?"

"Naw, I'm good, bro."

"A'ight."

I continued to smoke my blunt when my phone rung again, this time it was an unsaved number.

"Hello?"

"Hey, Chris."

"What's up, Unique?" I said, noticing her voice off back.

"I was calling to inform you that I'm getting a DNA test done with Yatta next week."

"I don't know what for, you already know it's mine."

"To try to get on good terms with him again."

"How is that? Because when the test comes back that he's not the father then what's the next step?"

"We just gone have to force shit. I know some of his traps and codes and you should know some too, we can get all that shit."

"Well, knowing a nigga like Yatta, he's always two steps ahead on the business tip. That shit probably moved somewhere else and them codes probably changed too. I tried to go in some traps he had but that shit was vacant."

"Well I will figure something out."

"Cool, how is my baby doing?"

"It's fine."

"True that, well call me and let me know what you come up with. You the one that was living with the nigga, you gotta think of something."

"Okay."

Hanging up the phone I finished my blunt then got myself together so I could make some money for the day. I just couldn't wait for the day we hit Yatta's ass. I'd probably just say fuck it and organize a plan with my cousin, Man Man.

Kenyatta

Sitting at the organization table with Jay and a few other little niggas that worked for me, I planned out how I was going to start going about things. I moved all of my traps to one big ass trap warehouse on the south side, and that's what this meeting was about.

"So everyone likes how the business is running?"

"Yeah, we straight," they all said in unison.

"This meeting is to let y'all know I moved the traps into one big ass warehouse out in the hundreds. Now I don't want no one else knowing this shit because I'm only telling y'all ass. No one else knows about this shit except for the ones in this room today, and that's how it's gone stay, understand?"

"Yeah," they all said at once.

"I got a question, Yatta."

I turned to look at Dee, who was only sixteen years old, but been doing this shit since he was thirteen.

"What's up, Dee?"

"Why you move the traps in the first place?"

"Too many motherfuckers know shit that I don't want them knowing. Is there any more questions?"

Everyone looked around the room at each other and shook their heads no.

"A'ight, so get back to making money. This meeting is dismissed."

Everyone got up and left the office which was in a spot I purchased a while back just to come chill in. After everyone left, Jay stood next to me.

"What's good, Jay?"

"Shit, I want to discuss something with you real quick."

"And what's that?"

"I talked to Chris the other day and he was asking me when you was gon' put him back on?"

"That nigga never getting back on my team. I heard her was selling for that nigga, OJ, so let that nigga stay where he at. You need to stop associating with that nigga."

"I got you."

Jay nodded his head then walked out of the office. It was bad I had to do Chris that way, but that nigga can't be trusted. It seemed off for Jay to ask me about that shit when he knew damn well I kept information between him and I for a reason. I wasn't no dumb nigga and I could sense snake shit going on, so I will just keep my eyes open on everybody. Shit yo' day ones be the first ones to cross you and I wasn't with that shit.

I laid on the bed in the next room and called Khadijah knowing her ass was at work, but she would still pick up for me.

"Hey, baby."

"What's up sweetheart, what time you get off today?"

"Um, probably early today because my last client needed a sew in and you know that don't take me long to do."

"True, you and little man can come over to my spot to chill if you want to."

"I like the sound of that. I'll let you know when I clock out."

"Okay, cool."

"Bye, baby."

"Bye, sweetheart."

I hung up and left my spot so I could go to my crib to straighten up a bit. It was only three-thirty so I knew it would be enough time to clean that big ass house and still go pick Dijah and little man up. Two hours later I got the house cleaned up and was about to take a shower 'til my doorbell rang.

"Who is it?"

I scrunched my face up because no one normally rings the bell. I live in a white neighborhood so nobody fucked with me. Reaching for my gun, I looked through the peephole and saw it was Unique's ass. I opened the door and stood in the way so she couldn't walk in.

"What?" I asked her, getting pissed off all over again just by looking at her.

"I want to know if I could come in and talk to you about things."

"Ain't shit to talk about. The DNA testing will be soon, so ain't shit needed to be said between us."

"I just want to let you know I still love you and I'm sorry for the pain I've caused you."

"Yeah, yeah, bullshit. Yo' ass wasn't loving me when you let the next nigga nut in you, so get the fuck from around my place. Just let me know when yo' ass going to the doctor so I can pay for the shit."

Before she could say anything else, I slammed the door in her face and watched her walk off to her friend's car as she drove off. That bitch needed to keep her distance for real. I wasn't a woman beater, but I would beat the shit out of her because she did some foul shit to me. I hopped in the shower then threw some clothes on and headed to Khadijah's job.

"Baby, I'm outside."

"Okay, here I come."

A few seconds later her beautiful ass walked out of the salon looking sexy as fuck. I loved how she kept her hair curly, it was so long down her back. Her hips and thighs had me so gone in a daydream that I didn't even notice her get in the car.

"Um, what's up with you?"

"I'm sorry, baby, you just so fucking beautiful to me."

She placed her hand over her heart then smiled.

"Thank you, baby."

"No problem."

"You don't have to worry about picking Jr. up, my sister is going to keep him for the weekend."

"Mm, so it's just you and me?" I asked licking my lips.

"Yup, just you and me."

"You know how we get down."

"Boy, shut up and drive. I want to see your place already."

I looked away from Khadijah then began driving. When we arrived, her mouth was wide open and she hadn't even step foot in the house yet.

"Oh my God, baby, it's beautiful!"

"Wait until you go inside."

I opened the front door and she walked ahead of me with her hand over her mouth looking at my large house.

"Yatta, I'm so mad at you!"

I smiled then looked her way.

"Why you mad at me?"

"Because all the time you been talking to me and I never got to see this place, it's so beautiful." She said as she walked upstairs to see the rest of the house.

Overall, I had three full bathrooms and five big ass bedrooms. I really loved this place and got it for Unique since she fell in love with it at first sight. Sitting back watching Khadijah's ass look through the house excited made me smile inside. Too bad I wasn't keeping this place any more. When Khadijah and I make it official, I'm moving her into something better.

"What's up?" I answered my phone while stepping out in the back.

"Yatta, you know damn well what's up."

"Gabby, don't start that bullshit. I told you I was coming out there next week, I ain't forgot about you."

"Fuck you mean, you ain't forgot about me? Nigga, I can't tell the way you ain't been talking to me."

Gabby was this older bitch I fucked with when I did business out of town. I met her ass like four months ago. Only reason I started fucking with her was because her city is where my connect stayed, so when we had to conduct business I would spend time down there with her. She's someone I could easily cut off because the bitch was just somebody I fucked after my business was done.

"Look, I'm not about to converse with you about this shit right now, I'm busy. I will see you when I see you."

73

I hung the phone up and walked back into the house while locking the door and saw Khadijah going through the refrigerator.

"You hungry?"

"Yeah."

"I'm going to run to grab something to eat real quick, what do you want back?"

"Get me a large Jim Shoe and a strawberry pop."

"Okay, baby. I'll be right back, it won't take that long."

We kissed before I left and went down the street to sandwich shop. I could see us together in a big house, being happy and most importantly, being the family that I've always wanted.

Chapter Ten

Unique

Since I was too early in my pregnancy to get the test done, they told me to wait until I was five months. So here I am, five months pregnant, waiting to get this damn DNA test over with. However, after reading up on it about having cramps and bleeding, I decided to just wait until the baby was born. Hopefully God does me right and it turns out to be Yatta's baby because Chris's broke ass was starting to piss me off acting like I couldn't come around and he's been ignoring my call.

Being pregnant and single was so awful. Especially at nighttime. Yatta completely cut me off, he even blocked the number I was calling him from which was Tasha's phone. I just didn't know what to do anymore and that's why I decided to hit the club with Tasha and a few other girls she knew. After showering and getting dressed in a strapless dress, I decided to put on my five-inch heels and flat ironed my hair which was growing out of control, but I loved it.

"Bitch, you know you don't need to be going to no damn club at five months pregnant."

"It's the only way I can get my mind off things. I don't have shit else to do."

"I guess, chick."

When we were done getting ready, we headed to the club. I know going to the club while pregnant is kind of ratchet but I would be going crazy if I stayed my ass in that damn house another night.

Tonya

After waiting for my mother's nurse to arrive, I got in my car and headed home. Chris had been talking to me since I've been gone and I really appreciated that so much. The little things he does makes me feel like a spoiled newborn. After I made it to my place, I noticed Chris was gone so I jumped in the shower and got dressed for the night. Dijah and I were going out to kick it at the club and catch up on old times.

I missed my chick; her and I were so close people always swore we were sisters. Dijah was like my diary, I would tell her everything. When I was nine I was raped by one of my mom's boyfriends and I was depressed for the longest time, but Dijah was right by my side every step of the way. Even though the man never got caught because my mom was too afraid to press charges on him, I can still remember his face clear as day. Every time I think about what happened to me I get upset all over again. My mother and I even fell out, our relationship was practically non-existent. I'm her daughter, and she was supposed to protect me no matter what. My phone started to ring as I put my hair up into a neat bun.

"Hey boo, you ready?" I asked.

"Yeah, did you want me to come get you or you coming to get me?"

"I will come to you, I'm about to leave out now."

"Okay."

After I hung up the phone, I sprayed some Bath and Body Works perfume on then got my things before I locked up and headed over to Khadijah's place. When I arrived I saw her on the porch talking to Kenny and it looked as if the conversation wasn't going well. After I parked my car, I began to walk over to them. Looking at Dijah, her ass was sitting right in the high waist, blue jeans and her breast were sitting at attention in her blue crop top. On her feet were a pair of black Gucci, T-strapped high heels, and her hair was flat ironed bone straight. K was looking like a brand new woman and I loved it.

"Aye, everything good?"

"Yeah, Tee, I'm good. Kenny's ass was just leaving."

I watched Khadijah's eyes that were fixed on Kenny. He then turned and looked at me.

"What's up, Tonya, how you and Chris doing?"

I rolled my eyes at him because I didn't want Dijah to know about me and Chris yet.

"We good."

He had a grin on his face as he looked at me.

"That's good to hear. Aye, Dijah, I'm coming to get my son this weekend so have him ready."

"Once again, you're not coming to get shit, so don't even bother to pop yo' ass up at my place Friday, Kenny. I'm not playing, you can't follow my instructions so you're not getting him, simple."

"Okay, well we'll see what the courts say. You want to go out dressed like these old, nappy-headed ass, hood rats, and have my son with your sister so you can go out. What type of hoe shit is that?"

"Watch yo' motherfucking mouth. I have my son with me at all times unless I'm working and sometimes he's with me there too. You haven't seen your son since he's been born. He will be two soon, and you think I'm going to just let you up and take my baby for a weekend when he don't even know you! That's a fuckin' shame how your own son hasn't seen your fuckin' face, but you out playing step daddy to the next bitch's kids. Go ahead and take me to court just to embarrass yourself because you ain't shit!"

"Yeah, whatever, you still love me though!" Kenny yelled back as he walked off the porch and to his beat up car and drove off.

"You sure you good, Dijah?"

"Yeah, I'm good. That nigga just slow as fuck. I wish he would just drop dead already."

We walked over to my car and got in.

"I'm loving that sundress though, Tonya, all that ass!"

We both laughed than I began to drive off while I handed Dijah a blunt to spark up. After she took a few hits off it, she passed it to me as we rode to Lauryn Hill's *Ex-Factor*. When we reached our destination, we were high as a kite. My cousin, Pouchie, worked the door so we got in quick. We made our way to the VIP section and swayed back and forth to Rihanna's song *Work* while sipping on some Apple Cîroc. I was only getting one cup because I had to drive us back.

"So how are things with you and Chris?"

"Its fine, we been good. I been meaning to tell you but since your big mouth, baby daddy told all my business, we been together for like two years now."

"Two years! That's crazy, I would have never thought you two would start a relationship."

"Yeah, that's my baby. How are things with you and Yatta?"

"Girl, it's okay. He and his fiancé broke up because she was cheating on him and got pregnant."

"Are you serious?"

"Girl, yeah. That bitch was tweaking, but I'm gone show her how a real woman's supposed to treat his ass."

Dijah swung her hair back at the last part and we both bust out laughing.

"How's your mother been, Dijah? She was always so nice to me whenever we had girl's night and stuff."

"She's good, she was helping me with a lot until I got on my own and shit. I was working up at this strip club and she hated me for a cause of it, but she got over it."

"The hell you was doing stripping and shit?"

"I had nothing, Tee. Literally nothing. After I had Jr. my mom paid for the apartment I'm living in now. She was paying the rent and bills so that's why I started to strip, you know. I didn't want my mom doing that for me, even though I was thankful she was doing it. Kenny's ass wasn't helping me with shit so I had to do what I had to do for me and my baby."

"I feel you, shit it's not easy out here raising a child by yourself."

"Hel naw it ain't. How's your mom doing?"

"We haven't spoken to each other for a minute, but I just came from over her house today. She's okay, she has a nurse staying there with her now. Sometimes I just really hate her."

"Why Tee? That's still your mother."

"Every time we talk or when I go around to check up on her, she always bring up the fact that I ran her boyfriend away from her. I got tired of that shit, so I stopped talking to her. "

"Well, some mothers don't mean what they say sometimes. She still loves you, though, no matter what."

"Girl, I don't feel it at all from her."

"It will get better, Tee."

After I sipped my drink, I peeped some pregnant chick making her way over to us with some thick chick right behind her. Khadijah and I exchange eye contact as the pregnant chick got closer.

"Aren't you the female I caught in Yatta's car a few months back?"

"Yeah, why?" Khadijah stood up and I stood up right beside her as the pregnant chick's friend got close.

"I just want to know are y'all in a relationship?"

"That's none of your business, why don't you go ask Yatta that."

"Listen, I'm trying to be as nice as I can because last I recall, I was still with him while y'all was fuckin' around."

"And last I recall, he got rid of your ass because you were cheating and got popped off by another nigga."

I watched as the pregnant female turned to her friend with wide eyes as if it was supposed to be a secret, then she turned back to Khadijah.

"For your information, this is Yatta's baby I'm carrying and as far as you, you're going to respect me. Wasn't you shaking and selling ass for money to provide for you and your son? And don't get it twisted, I know who yo' baby daddy is so keep that in mind."

"Bitch, I don't give a fuck about you knowing who Kenny is. Shit every female in Chicago know who that slut is, sad to say. You saying it like he gone beat my ass. Shorty I'm a grown ass woman. Yeah I was shaking my ass for money, but never sold ass so get your facts straight. And yeah, you can thank Yatta that I'm not shaking ass on the pole no more because he helped me get a job at his cousin, Keshia's salon."

After Dijah set that bitch straight, her and her friend started to walk off mugging us.

"This ain't over bitch."

"You lucky you pregnant, bitch because I would beat yo ass right now."

"It's only a matter of time. Yatta's gonna stop fuckin' with you and come back home to me just know that sweetie."

"What home do you own?"

Khadijah started laughing out loud after she asked the question, and the female couldn't answer it so she just walked away looking salty. What the hell was she even doing at a club pregnant anyway?

"Yooo, Dijah, who the hell was that?"

"Girl, that's Yatta's ex-fiancé I was just telling you about. That hoe just mad because she know she fucked up."

"Then got the nerve to come in here, belly all types of big, just ratchet. And how the hell she know your baby daddy?"

"Girl, I don't give a fuck. Let's get up out of here before I end up behind bars tonight."

We got up, left and went back to my crib for the rest of the night to kick it and chill like old times. I missed my best friend.

Kenyatta

"Why the fuck would you even do some shit like that, Gabby!"

"Baby, I want you to move out here with me. You don't even have to go back to Chicago."

"I'm going back to Chicago, I'm not staying out here with yo' ass. I have a girl and a son back home, I'm not about to be sitting here with yo' ass!"

I was highly pissed that Gabby's desperate ass burned my ticket for my flight back home while I was sleep. This bitch done lost her entire mind if she thought I was staying out here with her.

"Oh, so you have a son now? By who, that bitch, Unique?"

"Hell naw, don't worry about it."

I texted Jay's ass to send him to get me a new airport ticket. He came down with me because the connect wanted to let us know he was retiring and some other cat he trusted was taking over so we had to meet him. He seemed cool, he didn't seem like he was on no snake shit.

"Why can't we have a baby together?"

"Did you not just hear me?"

"Okay, so what you have a son. You could go visit him."

I got up and started to walk towards the bathroom because this bitch was pissing me off. I didn't understand how she was thirty-nine but still had the mindset of a teenager. After closing and locking the door, I turned the shower on and called Khadijah.

"Hey baby, how you doing?"

"I'm good, how are you?"

"I'm good, can't wait to see you and little man."

"When are you coming back?"

"It'll probably be either later on tonight, if not we leaving early morning."

"Okay, well I want you to be careful."

"You know I always am."

"Okay."

"I love you, Khadijah."

"I love you more, baby. Just let me know when you on your way back, hopefully it's gonna be tonight."

"Yeah, I hope so too."

"Okay, see you soon."

"Ok, baby. Bye."

"Bye."

After hanging up, I jumped in the shower and began to wash up. Drying off and getting dressed, I walked back into Gabby's room where she was sitting on the bed with her head down. Looking at her, I didn't know what made me fuck with her in the first place. I mean she was beautiful and heavy set, but she always wore fucked up ass weaves, and she has a childish ass mindset. I already told her what was up before we even started fucking around. My mind was gone when I started fucking around with her ass. I couldn't wait to get back home to my baby, Khadijah and our boy.

"Can I talk to you, Yatta?"

"About?"

"Well, I'm four months pregnant."

"Man, what the fuck!"

I slid down to the floor grabbing my dreads and held my head down. If I wanted to start a life with Khadijah, I had to find a way to get rid of this problem.

"Look man, you can't have this damn baby. No, I'm not having this shit at all."

"I'm having this baby, and you're going to be here for it every step of the way."

I stood up, glaring at her as I towered over her.

"You giving that baby up for adoption because I'm telling yo' ass right now, if you continue to go through with this pregnancy, you won't ever hear from me again. I promise you that."

"So you want me to get rid of our baby? A baby that you and I made together, a product of our love. You want to just kill it off like that?"

"You talking about love, I don't love you. I never said anything to you about loving you, so I don't know where you get that shit from."

"So guess what, whether you love me or not, I'm having this baby. And whether you want to be there or not, trust and believe this baby will be straight without your ass!"

"A'ight, bet."

I got out of her face then grabbed my things and headed over to Jay's hotel room. After Jay arrived, he opened the door and handed me my ticket as I made sure the door was closed all the way. Sitting at the table next to the mini kitchen, I held my head down and Jay came to sit next to me.

"What's bothering you, bro?"

"That bitch Gabby pregnant, and she saying she keeping it."

"Damn bro, you better hope she don't do no pop ups when we go back home, she looked like the crazy type."

"Man, we have to get rid of her."

"What you mean, like kill the bitch?"

"That's exactly what I mean."

"Shit, I'm down."

"A'ight, we gotta do that shit tonight before we leave. Make sure you call up Victor so he can have the jet ready for us. If we do this tonight, we need to get out of here quick."

"A'ight, I got you."

As Jay set up the jet for us tonight, I looked at Khadijah's picture on my home screen. All I could do was think about her and our future. Shit I was really falling for her because God put her in my life for a reason. With all that shit that happened with Unique's ass, it seemed as he placed her in my life right on time, and no one was going to fuck it up.

Chapter Eleven

Jay

After Yatta came up with the plan to kill Gabby, he's been going crazy. It was now six-thirty, and we were both dressed in all black, ready to get this shit over with. Yatta's my boy and all, but I honestly think he's going a bit too far with killing Gabby. Although she's pregnant with his baby, I still feel he shouldn't go through with this. I know I was down at first, but deep down I know he didn't want to do this. He's so far gone in the head over, Khadijah, that he's going insane. I never seen him act this way about Unique while they were together.

"Here, hold this."

Yatta handed me a shotgun while he held a butcher knife in one hand and a Uzi in the other. before he could reach the door, I grabbed his shoulder.

"You sure you want to go through with this?"

"Yeah, nigga, I been said I want the shit done. Fuck you keep asking me for?"

"Because Yatta, she is carrying your child. I know right now you want it done because you don't want Khadijah to find out, but years from now you gone regret this shit."

"Jay, man, I'm good on all that you talking 'bout. Gabby knew what the fuck it was, I believe her ass poked a hole in the condom or something. Ain't no way she's supposed to be pregnant bro, so like I said, I'm not gone regret shit that I'm about to do. May the Lord forgive me for my sins and what I'm about to do, but I can't deal with this shit, man!"

I watched Yatta fall down to the floor putting the gun and knife down and putting his hands over his face.

"Man, I just don't want Dijah to find out. I wanted to start a new life with her."

"I understand bro, but it's not like you got her pregnant while you were with her. You met gabby way before Khadijah was even thought of."

"I know, I just don't know how to break this shit to her. I mean, I don't want to leave my seed hanging, but damn man."

I walked over to Yatta, bent down to his level, and held my hand over his shoulder.

"Look, everything gone work out. Trust and believe me when I say this because everything happens for a reason, you said you always wanted a baby, right?"

He nodded his head.

"Well God just blessed you with two on the way."

"What you mean two? That shorty Unique carrying ain't mine."

"What you mean it ain't yours?"

"I caught her ass texting another nigga and they were discussing shit about the baby. I even asked her was it mine and she said she don't know. So I been waiting on her to get this DNA test done, but I guess she don't want it done because I haven't heard from her since."

"Damn, are you serious?"

"Hell yeah, fuck that bitch."

"Man, I never have thought Unique would do some shit like that, that's crazy bro. Well, at least you have a baby on the way."

"I'm just gone have to co-parent with her, and if she still on that goofy shit then I'm gone take my baby away from her ass."

"True."

I got a text from Victor saying the jet would be here soon. Yatta and I packed everything up and made sure we didn't leave anything behind before we headed out the door.

Khadijah

"Word around town is that you got that bitch nigga around my son."

"Nigga, don't worry about who I have around my child. Yo' ass ain't around, so miss me with that bullshit. You might as well say you don't have a son."

"Look, don't have that thug ass nigga around my son. That nigga is bad news."

"Kenny, worry about yourself. Bye."

With that being said I hung my phone up, blocking his number. Since Yatta's been out of town, Jr.'s been asking me questions about him. But the crazy part is he refers to him as his daddy. I was shocked when he first asked me, "where's daddy". I know he and Yatta have a good bond, but I didn't think he would call him daddy.

As I began fixing up my apartment there was a knock at the door.

"Who is it?"

"Yours truly."

I smiled at Yatta's crazy ass, but hearing his voice so close again made my heart beat faster. I unlocked my door and jumped right into Yatta's arms. He carried me inside and locked the door behind him as I started kissing on him from his mouth, down to his neck, and then up to his cheeks.

"I missed you so much, baby."

"I missed you too, sweetheart."

Yatta put me down and we walked to my bedroom and sat on my bed.

"What you been up to?"

"Just working and taking care of Jr. How'd your meeting go?"

"It went decent. When you gone get little man name changed?"

"I don't know about that Yatta, he's used to that name."

"That's true."

"But guess what he came and asked me the other day?"

"What?"

"He asked me where you were, but called you daddy."

"You playing?"

"I'm not, I'm so serious. I was looking at some of your pictures and he asked me, 'where is daddy at', while pointing to your picture."

I could tell he was happy because he had a big ass smile on his face.

"That's what's up, I told you that's my little man. Where is he at anyway?"

"He's in his room taking a nap."

"Okay, well I have to talk to you about some things. You gotta promise me you won't get mad, baby."

"Okay, I promise, what is it?"

"While I was with Unique, I met this chick out of town. Her name is Gabby and I was messing around with her for a while. When I went for my business meeting, she told me she was four months pregnant."

My heart dropped and felt like it was smashed into a billion pieces, but I didn't let him see that. Not only was Unique possibly carrying his baby, but now so was another chick from out of town and he went to go see her while he was out there. I wasn't the type to judge a person because who was I to judge, but the decision was up to me to deal with him and his baby mamas and a part of me didn't want to.

"Why Yatta?"

"Why what?"

"Why do you want to be with me? I mean, I have strong feelings for you but this shit seems like we as a couple isn't going to work."

"What you mean, why I want to be with you? When I first met you, there was a spark inside of me telling me you were the one for me. I know it seems like I got too much going on, but I promise you, we will get through this shit together. I don't want you to leave me, Dijah. I really do care about yo' ass."

I looked at him and he looked at me and as we sat in silence.

"You can't keep your dick in your pants, and on top of that you clearly don't like condoms so how the fuck do I know you won't cheat on me? It's too many STDs for you to be going in females raw. You were probably just out there with her, fucking her."

"No, Dijah, I wasn't. I promise you I won't cheat on you, take my word. She must have poked some holes in the rubbers because I always strapped up with shorty."

I stared at him, giving him the *yeah, okay* look.

"I didn't get a chance to tell you that me and your baby mama exchanged words at the club a couple of days ago."

I watched as he made a frown.

"What she say to you?"

"Basically said you're going to go back to her, y'all gone be a family, and you don't really want. Talking out the side of her neck."

"She's starting to work my last fuckin' nerve. I don't understand how she did wrong and knows she did wrong, but wants to continue to fuck with me. I gotta holla at her ass quick, and what the fuck was she doing at a club? She like five months pregnant and shit."

I watched Yatta shake his head in disgust at how ratchet his baby mama was.

"And her stomach big as hell for her to just be five months."

"Crazy part is, she ain't said shit else about the DNA test, so I'm guessing she don't want one."

"You can just get one when she has the baby."

"True, I most definitely will. When we gone start our family?"

Yatta pulled me onto his lap with a smirk on his face, like what he just said was funny or some shit.

"Um, you shouldn't be worrying about starting a family. All these kids you are expecting, you shouldn't be worried about having a baby with me."

"I want a baby by you, you have my heart."

"It's only been a few months, Yatta, stop it."

"Yeah, I know, but it feels like forever to me. God placed you in my life for a reason, and in my heart I feel it's because He knows you are my soulmate."

"Yeah, it sounds good. What if I'm not your soulmate?"

"You are my soulmate."

Yatta grabbed my hand and placed it over his heart. He had his hand on mine and as we sat in silence I felt that our heart beats matched one another. That shit was scary because I never felt that with no one, well never with Kenny.

"I love you, Khadijah."

"I love you too, Yatta."

We laid back on my bed and drifted off to sleep.

Unique

I laid back on the bed inside of the ultrasound room and pulled my shirt up as I waited for the doctor to put the jell onto my belly. I had to go to this appointment alone because Tasha had to work. Tasha has been going to all my doctor visits with me and that's why I loved my best friend.

"So, today you will be finding out the sex of your baby if you want to know."

"Yeah, I would love to know. I've been waiting for this day."

I watched as the black, female doctor turned a small screen in front of me and looked onto the big screen on the wall in front of her which had the same images on both. After typing information into the computer, she cut the lights off and began putting the cold jelly onto my stomach. She started moving the handle around, snapping pictures of the baby to see how it's development before she began to look for the sex of the baby. My baby was so stubborn it didn't even want to show me it's sex, but finally let the doctor see.

"You're having a baby girl!"

I smiled and tears came from my eyes as I watched my baby girl on the screen.

"Can I get 3D pictures of her, Doc?"

"Sure, no problem."

Just when she was about to snap the 3D pictures another head was seen behind my baby girl.

"Oh my God, please don't tell me that's what I think it is?"

"Yes, it is, you're having twins! Wow, congratulations Ms. Smith!"

"Thank you."

At this point I wasn't prepared to get the news that I was having twins. Every appointment went well without them noticing another baby inside of me. I guess it was doing some good hiding in there. The doctor did her best to snap pictures of the second baby and see how it was growing. She told me everything was developing well on Baby B as she began looking to identify the sex.

I waited patiently as I watched my babies move around, and finally the doctor announced it was a boy. I was so happy after my appointment was over and I walked out on cloud nine with 3D ultrasound pictures of my babies. As I waited for the bus to head back home, I looked at both the facial features and noticed my baby girl's face resembled more of Yatta and my baby boy's face resembled more of Chris. My heart started to beat fast as the thought of my babies having two different fathers crossed my mind. I never thought it could happen, or maybe I was just tripping, but I hope both my babies turned out to be Yatta's.

I waited five more minutes at the bus stop 'til the bus arrived and I rode it all the way back to the house. Good thing I only had to ride one bus because I was feeling sick to my stomach with my mind still stuck on the fact that my twins could have different fathers. After making it home, all I did was lay down and stare off while holding my stomach.

Chris

"Look, we need to just go through with this shit and get it over with. I'm tired of waiting."

I stressed to my oldest, first cousin Man Man.

"You can't just go through like that. You have to have a plan first so we don't fuck up."

"Man look, a nigga over here starving. I don't want his ex bitch to get shit out of me. I was just using her ass to get information for me, but since she got pregnant with my baby and her dumb ass didn't erase the messages he looked through her phone and kicked her ass to the curb. Knowing him, he not gone take her ass back so she's useless right now."

"Damn, you fucked up by getting that bitch pregnant, though."

"I already know."

"A'ight, well take a few more days and figure out how we going to set this shit up. I'm not trying to prolong this shit, but we have to do this shit right."

"I bet if we snatch that new bitch he with, he would up anything at that point."

"Nigga, hell naw, his ass would kill us and get the girl back easily. Yo' ass know this nigga don't play so stop coming up with bullshit ass plans. You don't know where he handles his business at?"

"He got this barbershop his granddad left him. I doubt he still conduct business in there though."

"Well I'll figure the shit out after I get word around the street and let you know what's up."

"A'ight, bet."

"Bet."

After my cousin got up and left I locked my door back and laid back on the couch to get my head together. I had to come up with a way to get this nigga and every single dollar he has.

Chapter Twelve

Khadijah

I was in the middle of packing when I heard banging on my door and my doorbell going off. It was nine in the morning and luckily, my son was at my sister's house and Yatta was gone to do business. I walked to the door with a frown on my face thinking if it was Kenny, I was going to treat the fuck out of him. When I opened the door my mouth dropped open as I stood there staring at my cousin on my father's side. I haven't heard from her since I got pregnant with Jr., and our last encounter was not pleasant.

"What do you want, Mary?"

"Can I come in and talk to you?"

I wasn't no petty, tit for tat person, so I let her in. When she sat on my couch, she looked around and then her big, brown eye balls reverted back on me.

"So, why are you here?" I asked getting to the point because I have a lot of packing to do since Yatta didn't want me staying here anymore.

"Well it's nice to see you too, cousin."

"Yeah, it is, now what do you want?"

"To be honest, Dijah, I have nowhere to go and I need a place to stay until I can get back on my feet again."

I looked at her with shock, here she was in the same position I was in just a year and a half ago. The crazy part about it is that when my mom forced me to move out of her place and I turned to my cousin for help, she straight dissed me. So I'm clueless as to why in the hell she was sitting in front of me looking a hot ass mess with bags and shit in her hands.

"Well, well, you know one thing about them tables? They always turn, don't they?"

"I know, and I'm sorry I dissed you like that, but you have to understand I was living with my man and I couldn't have you staying there."

"Fuck that supposed to mean? You thought I was gone sleep with your man or some shit?"

"It wasn't that, it's just that I didn't want females around the house when I wasn't around."

"That's cool. Well I'm moving in with my man, so you gone have to find somewhere else to go."

"I can't get in touch with no one else in the family, you're all I have."

"Well, you can go to Angel's house."

"When you moving?"

"Soon as I pack everything up."

"So it's like that now, Dijah?"

"Yup."

"Well what's her address?"

I wrote down Angel's address and phone number for Mary before I sent her on her way. After six hours of packing, I was finally done. I called Yatta to let him know I was finished and he said he was on the way.

Kenyatta

"Call somebody up to come clean this shit up, I gotta go," I said to Jay.

"I got you, but aye, you be careful, bro."

"You know I'm not worried about a damn thing."

I was running late getting to Khadijah because I had to body a disloyal ass nigga on my team. Caught his ass stealing out my stash of pills, so I had to off him real quick. I don't know why niggas try to test me like they ass won't get murked. I cut his hands off, put them in a Ziploc bag, and planed on showing them to the guys at my next meeting.

I made note a note to have another meeting with the guys to show they ass if one more slip up happened, I wouldn't have no hesitate bodying they ass.

As I pulled in front of Khadijah's place, I parked my car and made my way up the steps. Noticing the door was open, I grabbed my gun and slowly walked inside seeing Dijah holding her head down while she cried.

"Baby, what's wrong? Why you have the door open?"

She looked at me and her eyes were a dark black color while tears ran down her face. Handing me some papers I scanned through them and saw that Kenny was trying to take her to court to get full custody of Jr.

"Baby, it's okay. Everything will be okay, I promise you that."

"How, Yatta? He's trying to get custody of my baby, Jr. don't even know him."

"Baby, you are the one that cared for him since an infant. You the one that makes sure he gets to his doctor appointments, has a roof over his head, clothes on his back, and food in his stomach. I'm cool with some lawyers down at the court, they like family, so just chill out. Don't stress about it because that deadbeat ass nigga ain't getting custody of shit."

"I'm just emotional right now because what if they order joint custody? I gave him chances to come over here to spend time with Jr., you know, so he can get to know him before he just up and take him without me being around."

"It's going to be okay, baby. Trust me."

I grabbed the back of her head and began kissing her then stood back up as she wiped her tears away.

"Are you done packing?"

"Yeah."

"Okay, grab your personal things with you so we can ride to the house. I will have my boys come pick up the boxes."

When we locked up and went out to the car, I couldn't help but smile at the fact that Khadijah didn't know she was going to be in a whole new mansion. It was further off by the suburbs so we picked Jr. up on our way there.

When we arrived Jr. was asleep, so I picked him up and carried him while I looked at a confused Khadijah.

"Baby, what is this? This is not the same place."

"I know, just open the door."

When she opened the door, she was in awe. She turned around and kissed me then turned back to the new house. Everything was furnished just the way she liked it. I looked around her old apartment and seen a couple of things that stood out like paintings, curtains, couches and things that she liked so I hired a decorator and she hooked it up to Khadijah's liking. As we walked in Jr. was awakened by his mother's screams of excitement which caused me to laugh at her being so dramatic.

"Daddy, what's wrong with mommy?"

"Nothing, she's excited about our new house."

I watched as Jr. rubbed his eyes and looked around the living room which had baby blue connected couches and a flat screen smart TV followed by a blue rug with a black woman holding a new born baby on it.

"This is my new house?"

"Yeah, little man."

He jumped in my arms as I put him down and he ran everywhere, then we went upstairs to where the bedrooms were. I showed little man his room, seeing that he liked Spiderman and Batman, I had the decorator paint his walls red, black, and yellow with the two characters standing above his Batman bed. In the corner were action figures, board games, Xbox games, and of course he had a flat screen. I watched as he ran over to the toys and grabbed them then started to play with everything. I went down the hall to our bedroom where I found Khadijah's sensitive ass crying on our queen sized canopy bed with blue and black curtains.

I walked over to her and sat next to her.

"What's wrong now, baby?"

"It's so beautiful. You have my favorite paintings throughout the house and our bedroom is beautiful. Hell, everything in this house is beautiful and complete. I love it and I love you. Thank you so much, baby."

"I love you more, baby, but you don't have to thank me. I just want to make sure our family is straight and to have enough room to make babies."

She gave me a death glare soon as I said that, but I started laughing.

"For real though, baby. I want kids by you, you see all this space. Plus they will be well taken care of."

"I know that much, but I don't want them to have siblings here and there."

"Shit, we gone have kids back to back. They will have more than enough time with each other here."

"I'm serious, Yatta."

"I got you, baby."

When the doorbell rang, I knew it was the movers so I opened the door and helped out with the boxes.

Chris

Watching Mary suck the skin off my dick had my head gone as I smoked on some Kush. Mary and I met a while back at a trap that she used to be in counting up money for the shorties who were selling weed. I stopped messing with her ass because I was getting serious with Tonya, but now knowing she's related to Khadijah I decided to start back fucking with her. I needed to see if I could get information about Khadijah which would give me information on Yatta's ass. As I filled her throat up with my seeds I got up and headed to her bathroom to wash my manhood off.

"Baby, when you gone come spend time with me? I'm tired of you coming and leaving."

After I was done I zipped up my pants and walked back into her bedrooms. Mary wasn't ugly, but compared to Tonya, Tonya had her beat. Mary was thick in the hips with a small waistline and a little bit of a pudge. Her rich, chocolate skin is what attracted me to her. I don't know why, but I love me some chocolate women.

"I told you I be busy. You got any information for me?"

"The day I showed up at her crib lying about needing a place to stay she didn't buy it. She was in the middle of packing and she told me she was moving in with Yatta."

"That's all you got?"

"Yeah, I told yo' ass she wasn't gone buy the shit cause of how I dissed her when she was pregnant."

I held my head down thinking of a way to get to Khadijah, so I decided to hit my bro up after I left.

"Baby, why are you trying to take Kenyatta out? You can start your own shit and be better."

I'm really not trying to hear that shit right now, Mary. I'm out."

I glanced over at Mary who now had a mug on her face and her arms crossed over her chest, but I ignored her ass and walked out to my car. Just when I was about to call my brother Kenny, Unique's ass was calling.

"What's up, Unique?"

"Nothing, I see you haven't been calling me no more."

"Don't even start that shit, I'm not in the mood."

"Well I found out what I'm having."

"And what's that?"

"A baby girl and a baby boy."

"What you mean a girl and a boy?"

"I'm having twins Chris, but I looked at the 3D pictures and the girl looks like Yatta and the boy looks like you."

"What? That shit ain't even possible, Unique."

"It is Chris, look it up."

Fuck! I cursed inside my head. I was gone have to hurry up and take this nigga out before she dropped them babies because knowing Yatta, his ass was gone want them DNA tests done soon as they came out. I was trying to get this shit done so I could hurry up and leave with Tonya before this shit got out.

"Have you talked to Yatta?"

"No, but Chris this shit has to stop. Whatever you plan on doing to him has to stop. If I'm carrying both of y'all babies, then you have to find a different way to make money because I want both of my children to have their father."

Before she could say anything else, I hung up on her. I was not in the mood to hear that shit. She knew what the fuck it was I was trying to do and she know ain't no stopping this plan. I need my money and that nigga dead.

"What's up, bro?"

"Shit man, what's up with you and your baby mama?"

"Shit, I'm taking her ass to court to get full custody of my son. She won't let me take him nowhere and I shouldn't have to go through this extra shit she talking 'bout, plus mama want to see him."

"True, yeah, I ain't seen my nephew in a minute. But aye, you heard she been messing around with that nigga Yatta and she moved in with him."

"No the fuck that bitch didn't move my son in with some other nigga. This bitch got me fucked up if she thinks my son living with that nigga is cool but I can't even get him when I want."

"Hell yeah, that's some crazy shit, bro. But holla at me a lil later, I want to discuss some shit with you."

"A'ight."

When I hung up, I drove back to the crib. I was happy today was Sunday because that meant Tonya's ass was off and I wanted to spend some time with my baby.

Chapter Thirteen

Tonya

"This place is so lovely, best friend!"

I walked around in awe. It was so big and I loved all of the black inspirational paintings that were up.

"I fell in love the first time. Yatta's ass was laughing at me, you should have seen me."

We sat in her living room while Jr. was sleeping in her arms.

"So, what's going on?"

"I'm going crazy right now."

"Why?"

"Kenny's trying to get full custody of Jr."

"Excuse me?"

"I know, right? But Yatta supposed to be handling that. Do you think they will still do joint custody if he doesn't get full custody?"

"I'm not sure, but if you tell them that he hasn't been around since he's been born they shouldn't give him anything. That's crazy though, I would be going crazy, too. Hell, Jr.'s about to be two in a month and now he wants full custody? He a trip."

"Right. It pisses me off every time I think about it."

"Girl, you gone be straight. You been getting some new clients?"

"Yeah, I got some back to school appointments lined up. What about you?"

"Yeah, they getting up there. So how you and Yatta been?"

"That's my baby! I mean I couldn't ask for anything better, he's what I been looking for in a man and I'm very thankful for him. But..."

"Don't tell me no bad news, I love y'all together."

"He got another baby on the way."

"He cheated on you?"

"No, he was messing around on his ex-fiancé with this one, she lives out of town."

"How many months is she? And how do you feel about this?"

"I think he told me four months."

"Wow, I wasn't expecting that. How do you feel about that?"

"Me either, but I mean I can't do nothing but accept it because it was before me and he's the man I want to be with so I would treat them kids no different. You should see the bond him and Jr. share, he started calling him daddy on his own."

"Aww, that's so cute. Well, I'm happy for you. Just take things one step at a time, there's always obstacles being thrown at you. It's all about how you handle them."

"Yeah, that's true. But it gets hard at times because he says he wants me to have his kids, but I'm like kids should be the last thing on your mind."

We both began busting out laughing.

"Girl, I know that's right. Shit his ass shouldn't be worried about no more babies for the next ten years."

"Okay."

We both laughed causing Jr. to jump in his sleep, so Dijah put him down on the couch next to us.

"Has your mom met him, yet?"

"No, she doesn't even know about him yet."

"Are you going to tell her about him?"

"Yeah, I might just invite him over to a dinner that she's having next week."

"I hope it goes well, have you met his mother?"

"No. Actually, since we been talking, he's never brought up his mother."

"Do you think he doesn't want you to meet her?"

"Honestly, I don't know, Tee."

"Maybe he's just trying to find the right time for y'all to meet, you know like you."

"Yeah, true. But how you been doing?"

"Girl, I been good. Nothing new been going on."

"What about you and Chris?"

"We been good."

"That's good. Has he been acting suspicious around you lately?"

"No, why you ask that?"

"You gotta promise you won't say anything to nobody."

"Okay, I promise."

"Yatta was saying something about him acting sneaky, like he been taking money on the side or something."

"That's crazy, he doesn't seem like he's doing anything to me but I will pay more attention to him now."

"Please don't mention anything like that to him."

"Girl I'm not, I got you."

After chatting it up some more with my girl, I had to head back home. The whole ride back home I was trying to think on how Chris been acting lately and I couldn't come up with anything. I made a mental note to myself to keep an eye on him.

Kenyatta

"You motherfuckers knew what he was up to, so why ain't nobody say shit!" I yelled at these niggas.

Looking at their asses, I could tell someone knew.

"So Nick, did you know he was taking my product on the side?"

I walked and got in his face. Only reason I walked to him was because he and Terrence were best friends.

"Yeah, I knew, but I tried to stop him plenty of times. He wouldn't listen man."

These young niggas been on my team selling for me since they were thirteen, but I already knew some shit like this was gone happen since their asses became seniors this year. Teenagers liked to party and get high, but not on my damn watch because I needed every dollar. I held out my hand so Jay could pass me the Ziploc bag.

When he handed it to me, I held it up so every last one of these young ass niggas could see it. They ass needed to know I wasn't the one to be fucked with.

"Take a good look at this shit! Anyone that feel they got the balls to steal from me again, I will make sure to body yo' ass and add your motherfuckin' hands to the collection! Do I make myself clear?"

"Yeah, boss," everyone said in unison.

"A'ight, now get y'all ass back out there and make my money."

I watched every single guy leave the room, but it was something about that nigga Nick. So after everyone the room was cleared I pulled him to the side. Nick and Terrence were like my little brothers. I hate that I had to end Terrence's life, but shit, he knew the consequences of crossing me.

"Sit down."

Nick sat down at the table and I sat across from him while Jay stood by the door.

"So what's been up with you?"

"Nothing, been making this money, you know, same shit."

"I know you about to be a senior this year, how you feel about that?"

"I'm proud of myself."

"Me too. I'm just gone get straight to it bro, I want nothing but the best for you. I don't want you out in these streets like the rest of these niggas, I want to see you become somebody."

"I hear you."

"You like a little brother to me man you know that?"

"Hell yeah, I been knowing you since I was thirteen."

"Yeah, you and Terrence."

When I said his name, Nick had a look on his face. It was partially sad, but more so concerned.

"Why Terrence steal from me?"

"He was taking some, but was also giving some to Chris's brother."

"What you mean by giving it to him?"

"He was giving it to him to sell on the streets."

I felt my blood began to boil.

"So why haven't you let me in on this?"

"I was afraid of what would happen."

"Well you see your friend gone, so if you ever think of doing some shit like that you will be reunited with him. And if you see or hear some more niggas doing the same shit, you let me know ASAP, or next time I won't spare your life."

"I got you, bro."

"Now on some other shit, when you start school I want you to come see me about a job so I can get you off of these streets and away from this lifestyle."

"Okay, good looking."

"No problem."

"Aye?"

"What's up?"

"You and Chris into it or some?"

"Not that I know of, why you ask?"

"Because I haven't been seeing him around lately, and I just told you he was giving his brother, Kenny some of your product to sell."

"Don't worry 'bout it, I'll look into it."

"A'ight."

When he left the room I turned to Jay.

"I know you heard that shit."

"Hell yeah, so what you want to do?"

"I'm gone pay Chris's ass a visit."

"You want me to come?"

"Naw, I got this," I said showing him my Uzi.

"Man, I never thought this day would come."

"Me either but sometimes shit like this happen. That nigga been acting funny before I even cut him out the deals."

"Well, you gotta do what you gotta do."

"Already know. I will hit you up though, bro."

I stood up and slapped hands with Jay and left out. Walking to my car flashbacks began crossing my mind of when Jay, Chris and I were kids. We always had this mentality that we were gone stick together because, shit we were basically brothers. I've seen this shit happen on TV and shit, but I never thought it would be one of my boys to cross me like this. I sent Dijah a text saying I wouldn't be picking her up from work tonight and headed over to the crib to change.

I threw on my black shirt, a pair of black jeans and black Timbs. I zipped my black hoodie up and headed over to Chris's spot.

I sat in his driveway and rubbed my head then wrapped my dreads to the back. The conversation Chris and I had back when we were teenagers came to my thoughts. Out of that conversation I got the vibe from him that he wanted to be on top. He wanted everything and anyone in his way was going to be dealt with. Back then I never paid attention to the shit he used to say because I never thought he would do some shit like this.

I put the Uzi in the back of my jeans, walked up to his doorstep and I rung his bell. A few minutes later the door opened and there stood Chris's snake ass with wide eyes.

"What's up? Can I come in and talk to you about some shit?"

I saw that he was hesitant at first, but then he let me in. I looked around the living room and spotted an ultrasound on a table by the door, but couldn't really get a good look at the name on top of it. After he locked the door he walked over to me.

"You can have a seat."

I sat on the chair that was in the living room and he sat across from me.

"So what's up, Yatta?"

"A few things."

"Like what?"

"Why you being a snake?"

"What the fuck are you talking about, man?"

I could tell he knew exactly what I was talking about just by reading his eyes which had fear in them.

"I know you been stealing money from me and I know for a fact you had your brother get one of my guys to bring him some of my new product so y'all could make money. But my question to you, is why the fuck would you cross me to begin with? I thought we were boys."

"Man, I don't know what the fuck you talking about."

"Okay, now you wanna play this role. How about you confess now and I spare your fuckin' life?"

I looked him dead in his eyes and he began to get nonchalant.

"Look at you. You got the money, you got the power over these streets. You know that was always my dream."

"I made sure you had just as much money as I did, you and Jay so what's really the issue?"

Just when I said that I heard heels coming from a bathroom and in walked Unique and her big ass stomach.

"Aw ok, I see how this shit go!"

I stood up and looked between the two in shock, but I wasn't surprised because I had my suspicions.

"It's not what you think, Yatta, I promise you!"

"Save your fuckin' breath! Chris, man this how we get down now! How long y'all been fucking?"

"We haven't—"

115

"Over a year now."

This nigga was bold today.

"That's what's up. So Unique you carrying that nigga baby?"

"Yes, Yatta but—"

I chuckled to myself at the fact I gave this bitch everything. Sad to say I loved her ass, and in return she got pregnant by my snake ass friend.

"It's crazy because I knew what was up. I just waited till the shit played out."

Chris stood up and walked towards me and started swinging but I ducked and punched him in the stomach, causing him to double over and Unique ran, or rather waddled out the house. I didn't give Chris a chance to get up because I kicked him in the head, causing him to fall back and I stood over him pulling out my gun, aiming it at his dome.

"Anything you gotta say?"

"Man look, I'm sorry, I wasn't thinking straight Yatta. This shit was not supposed to happen like this, man please don't kill me."

"You should have thought about the shit you been doing behind my back nigga!"

I squeezed the trigger and his blood and brains were all on the floor and walls. I ran back to my car leaving the scene. I drove down the street taking my hoodie off and placing my gun in my empty duffle bag. Heading down to Unique's friend's house, I spotted her disloyal ass on the porch crying and her friend consoling her. When I walked up to them both, had fear in their eyes. Tasha left and went inside the house without a word being said.

"What the fuck was your purpose, Unique!"

When I yelled it caused her to jump, so I had to calm myself down before I drew unwanted attention. She stood up from the step she was sitting on and looked me dead in my face.

"I love you, Yatta, I really do. It's just I felt I needed someone new, you know? I'm still young, I still wanted to explore."

"But with a man I called my friend, and for over a year? That's some spiteful shit to do, and to top it off you carrying the nigga's baby?"

"Yeah, but I'm carrying yours too."

"Fuck you mean?"

"I'm pregnant with twins. I had a 3d ultra sound done and one looks like you and the other looks like Chris."

"This shit is crazy man. Check this out, when you pop them motherfuckers out, you hit my line so I can get the test and shit done. Until then, yo' ass dead to me. Real talk, I fuckin' hate you for doing the shit you did to me, straight up."

I walked off on her causing her to scream my name, but I ignored her. I flamed me up a blunt while I drove off, heading home to take a shower and get ready to pick up Dijah.

Chapter Fourteen

Khadijah

"Hey, baby."

I kissed Yatta on the lips as I got in the car but he had an unreadable look on his face.

"Baby, what's wrong?"

I began putting my straight hair up in a ponytail then looked at him as he started the car up.

"We picking up Jr.?"

"My sister bringing him tomorrow night. What's wrong?"

"I have to talk to you about some things."

I put my seatbelt on then sat back in the seat as Yatta began driving to the house. The whole forty-minute drive was a long one, and Yatta did not say one word to me the whole time. When we arrived at the house, he unlocked the door, went straight to the kitchen cabinet, and grabbed a bottle of Hennessy. He began to drink straight from the bottle.

I gave him one last look before I walked upstairs to our room. Changing into some pajamas, I let my hair down and laid on the bed drowning in my thoughts of what could be Yatta's problem.

Just as I was about to turn the light out in walked Yatta with the bottle of Hennessy still in his hand. I watched as he sat the bottle down on the night stand and took off his clothes, down to his boxers. He walked over to the dresser and pulled out some basketball shorts then he walked to his nightstand, pulled out his swishers and his loud, and began rolling up. After rolling up four blunts and flaming up one, he finally sat next to me as he inhaled and exhaled the weed.

"I want to let you know first that I don't want to leave you. I love you, Khadijah and nothing's going to change that. I came across a couple of females and even been with one for damn near my whole life and this feeling that I have inside me for you, I've never felt. I see how you are with Jr. and it reminds me so much of how I use to be with my mother."

I looked at his face and he was so serious that it made me tear up a bit.

He passed the blunt to me after hitting it a couple more times then started to drink the Hennessy as I smoked the blunt.

"When I was seven years old, I watched my pops beat my mother to death."

I grabbed my chest with my free hand and sat the blunt inside the ashtray. I reached over and held on to Yatta who now had tears down his face.

"I'm so sorry to hear that, baby, I really am."

"I was so helpless. I couldn't do a damn thing to save my mother and it hurts me to know he's in jail, still breathing, while I will never get to see or talk to my mother again."

I began rocking Yatta back in forth in my arms as he let out his hurt and tears. I know men don't like to cry, but finding out his mother was murdered by his father and him breaking down had me in tears as well.

"Baby, it's going to be okay."

I wiped his tears away then wiped mine away.

120

"My boys were all I had since then. Jay and Chris, they were my brothers, and the funny thing about that is that it's always that one out the bunch to be on some snake shit."

"Which one?"

"I found out Chris and Unique was fucking around for a year and she's pregnant with that nigga babies."

"Babies?"

"She's having twins but saying one looks like me and the other looks like Chris."

"Wow."

I couldn't find a word to say after finding out Unique was pregnant with twins and they could have different fathers.

"I know you're hurting, baby, and I know you have a lot on your plate right now, but I'm willing to stick it out with you. I'm willing to ride with you 'til I can't ride no more, baby. I'm not going nowhere, I'm here for you every step of the way."

After I honestly told him that, he held my face in his hands as we gazed into each other eyes. Our lips met and when I say this kiss brought sparks through my body, I'm not lying. He laid me down on the bed then began to take my pajama pants off followed by my underwear. After I was staring at him in my birthday suit, he took his shorts and boxers off. Climbing on top of me. he started to kiss my neck then trailed the kissed down to my breast, sucking on my nipples. His kisses lowered to my stomach causing chills to come over me.

When he got to my womanhood, he kissed both my inner thighs then placed kisses on my now wet box causing me to moan. After a few more kisses, he began to go in. With him holding my hands down on the bed he began to feast on my treasure pot and it drove me crazy. We made eye contact as he licked, slurped, and kissed my pearl, causing my moans to become louder. When he let my hands go, I grabbed his head and began grinding my womanhood into his mouth which made me have the best climax ever.

When he got up with a smirk on his face, my mouth began to water as I watched him walk over to the closet to get a towel. As he wiped my juices off his face, I couldn't help but stare at his long, thick ten-inch manhood standing at attention. When he walked over to me, I bent down on the bed as he stood in front of me and I took all of him in my mouth.

I never gave head to anyone, but tonight I was going like a pro causing him to say all type of curse words and moan my name. He grabbed the back of my head and began pumping in and out of my mouth. I guess he felt his self about to cum because he pulled my head off his manhood.

"Damn, Dijah, almost made me nut. Turn your ass around for daddy."

I did as he instructed with a smile on my face. When I was comfortable, he smacked my ass cheeks hard then put himself inside me causing me to gasp.

"Shit, this shit feels so good, baby."

In response, I began to moan as he fucked me and pulled my hair.

"Whose pussy it is, baby?"

"It's yours."

"What's my name?"

"Daddy!"

He slapped my ass with his free hand and began to dig deep inside me, hitting my spot causing my legs to shake.

"I didn't hear you, what's my name, baby?"

The more he dug into me the louder I got. Between him pulling my hair and digging inside me my body was feeling a rush that I never felt before.

"Daddy!"

"Who you love?"

"I love you, Yatta!"

"Say this pussy only for me."

He smacked my ass harder.

"It's only for you, daddy! Ohhhh, Yatta I'm about to cum!"

"Come on."

He sped up, still giving me long, deep stokes. On his last stroke he and I both climaxed, causing me to fall flat on the bed trying to catch my breath. I could not move for nothing, so I just laid there breathing hard as I felt Yatta's lips kiss the back of my legs, then up to my ass, followed by kisses to the small of my back causing me to smile. He finally laid next to me and I turned over and to lay on his chest with my eyes closed.

"Dijah?"

"Yes, baby?" I asked with my eyes still closed.

"I love you."

"I love you, too."

He pulled me closer to him, making me feel loved and secure. Placing a kiss to my forehead, we both drifted into a deep slumber.

Tonya

When I arrived to my house after checking in on my mother, I had a feeling that something just wasn't right. I unlocked the door and stepped inside, then closed and locked it.

"Chris, baby, I'm home!"

It was dark so I figured he wasn't here. I turned on the lights and sat my keys on the table and an unwanted feeling came over me as I looked at an ultrasound picture with twins. The name said Unique but I didn't want to believe he was cheating on me. Carrying the ultrasound in my hand, I was pissed. Not only did this nigga have a bitch in our house, he got her pregnant too. I walked towards the living room and cut the light on. I immediately dropped the picture and placed my hands over my mouth looking at Chris, laying on the floor with blood splatter on the walls and brain matter everywhere.

Thinking someone was in the house, I grabbed the ultrasound and my keys and left. Driving with nowhere to go, tears began to cloud my vision so I pulled over at a gas station. I opened my car door and threw up everything I ate today. After I was done, I went inside the gas station and bought two bottles of water and went back out to my car. I opened one bottle and used it to rinse my mouth out and spat the residue on the ground. After repeating it twice, I threw the water bottle and got back in my car to drink the second bottle. I sat there and cried my heart out. I couldn't figure out who would want to do some shit like this to him. I wiped my tears then picked up my phone and dialed my best friend's number hoping she was up.

The phone rung and she answered on the third ring.

"Hey girl, what's up? I was just knocked out."

I could hear in her voice that she had just got up. With me being too chocked up to say anything I just cried in the phone.

"Tee, what's wrong? Where are you?"

I cried a few more minutes them got myself together as I finally spoke began to speak, thankful that she didn't hang up on me.

"He's gone, Dijah!"

"Who? Where are you!"

"Chris is dead!"

"Oh my God, where are you?"

"I'm in my car at the gas station down the street from my house. He's lying in the middle of the floor and it's blood everywhere. I don't know who would do this!"

"Calm down, calm down. Ride over to my place and you can spend the night. I'm going to wait 'til you get here. Hurry up, you don't need to be in that area."

"Okay."

I drove over to Dijah's place with my thoughts drowning me with question after question. Finally arriving at her place, she was waiting outside for me in her robe. I got out and walked over to her with her arms out, and I fell into them and cried. After I was done, we walked inside her house and sat on the couch. It was awkward because Yatta was sitting there as well with his head down.

"Look, it's some things I have to say to you, Tonya."

Yatta said to me looking at me.

"Okay."

"You found Chris dead and that was because of me."

"Oh my God! Why would you do that to him!"

"Let me tell you why, calm down."

Khadijah began rubbing my back.

"I found out Chris was stealing money from me and basically trying to get me out the way so he could take my spot. I also found out him and my ex fiancé was messing around for over a year, and she's pregnant with his twins. So I had to off his ass. Him and I were like brothers and I made always sure that nigga was straight, but for him to steal from me, plan to take me out so he could take my spot, sleep with my finance behind my back and get her pregnant? That nigga wrote his own death wish. I'm sorry for your lost, but that nigga was a snake and he had to go."

I was at a loss for words. Feeling a headache coming on, I just laid back on the couch and stared at the ceiling.

"It's going to be okay, best friend, I promise."

Those words my best friend said made me feel better, but I was still in shock that Chris was cheating on me for a whole year. How did I miss that shit?

Yatta got up and walked out the room leaving me and Khadijah to talk.

"How could he do that to me?"

"He's real petty for that shit. And Unique is the pregnant bitch I exchanged words with at the club."

"Yeah, I remember. This shit is crazy."

"Look at me."

I lifted my head up and looked at Dijah.

"I know you're hurting and I know you're pissed off right now, but you are going to overcome this. Trust me, things played out this way for a reason and he honestly got what he deserved. That was his karma for

126

cheating on you and fucking over one of his day ones. It will be okay, and I'm here for you."

"Thanks, best friend."

She got up and hugged me tightly then let go.

"It's a bedroom right by Jr.'s room so you can take that one. There's clean sheets and covers in there, just get you some rest. Do you need anything?"

"Yeah, I need some pain pills because my head is killing me."

"Okay, I'm going to get you some and a bottle of water."

"Okay, thanks so much."

"It's no problem."

I watched as Dijah walked up the stairs and I got up and walked to the bedroom I would be sleeping in tonight.

I opened the door and the bed was queen sized and looked so comfortable with purple and black sheets on it. I sat on the bed as Dijah walked in with some Tylenol and a water bottle. I took two pills and swallowed it down with water. Khadijah left the room and closed the door behind her. I took my shoes off, turned the lights out and laid down on the bed as my thoughts of Chris cheating on me caused my mind to wander. For a whole year he was messing around on me and I never knew, and that angered me. All I could do was cry myself to sleep.

Chapter Fifteen

Ken

"We gone track that nigga down and take him and his peoples out. It's just going to take some time."

I said to my homeboy, Rich, who been my day one since we were youngins. It's been two years since my brother Greg was killed in these streets. Don't get me wrong, I hadn't given up on finding who killed him. I came back to Chicago as soon as I got the information on the young niggas that did it.

Being back in Chicago brought back so many memories of what use to be. The moment I landed I felt a pain in my heart and wanted to turn back around. I thought of how my daughters Khadijah and Angel would look now. I left their mother when Khadijah was just three years old and Angel was five. That's when my brother, Greg stepped in to take care of them and make sure they were straight. I left Chicago because I wanted to better myself and that's exactly what I did. I own two restaurants out in Cali and a strip club so things for me were great. I just wish I would have moved my family out there with me.

"So how you gone get in touch with your daughters?"

"I have to find their mother. If she still lives in the same house then that will be no problem. You haven't heard anything from them?"

"I heard from a bird that Khadijah was striping down at the gentleman's club."

I shook my head at the fact that my baby girl was degrading herself and I blamed myself for it all. I should have taken them with me so they would've have a better life too.

"Alright, I'm going to get up out of here and find my kids man."

"Okay, be safe out here man."

"You must have forgot who I am Rich, we both ran these streets. These young niggas not on a crumb."

"You must don't watch the news, these niggas have no structure and don't care about who they shoot. It's babies and pregnant woman getting killed out here and you know back then that shit was not cool at all."

"Hell naw it wasn't, but these young cats don't scare me. I been there done that."

"A'ight, man."

When I walked to the car I got in and headed over to the kids' mother, Tracy's house. Feeling a bit nervous, I lit my cigarette and began to smoke it with my windows down. I just prayed and hoped she was still living in the same spot.

Tracy and I started dating when we were teenagers in high school. Although she lived in the suburbs at the time, I still made it my business to pick her up and drop her back off at a decent time. Her parents didn't like us together at all, so when we graduated we got our own place out in the city. Tracy was the only white girl I dated, and to be honest, I hate that I left her the way I did with two of my kids to raise. Back then, females use to be jealous of her because she was a beautiful, white woman with long, brown hair and had me, the hottest nigga in the city. Don't get me wrong, she held her own for a white woman, but I never let her fight in my site. I was the king of these streets and my family stayed straight.

I never cheated on Tracy. The main reason I left was to avoid getting locked up for murder that I committed a few weeks prior. I never contacted Tracy after I left and that was just me being a coward. I pulled out my thoughts when I pulled up to Tracy's house. I saw her sitting on the steps with her long, brown hair pulled up into a ponytail.

She looked well over 50 and that wasn't good. Stepping out of the car, I took my Chicago Bulls hat off and held it in front of me as I walked over to her.

Her green eyes got wide as she looked up at me then a few tears escaped them. She stood up and we just stared at each other; I could tell she was hurting inside.

"Why are you here, Ken?"

"I just want to check up on you and the kids."

"Kids? They both are grown ass women and have children of their own!"

"Look, let's go inside and talk."

Tracy still lived in our house in the suburbs. I purchased it for her on birthday years ago. The only reason I bought her this house was because I didn't want her being in the hood.

I watched her turn around and walk towards the door and I followed. Seeing how she redecorated the place I realized how much I really missed out on and it kilt me inside.

"Tracy, I'm sorry about everything. I had to leave, the police were after me."

"I am forty-three years old now, I've been just fine without you. You up and left your family, that was your choice, no one else's Ken."

She sat on the sofa and I sat down next to her. Looking around the room I could see pictures of Angel and Khadijah when they were younger.

"Do you have any recent pictures of them and my grandkids?"

"I don't understand why would you come back. You can continue to live how you been living, we don't care nothing about you."

"I understand that you're hurt, but those are still my daughters and I want to see them. It's never too late to be a father."

When I said that, she had a frown on her face and got up headed towards a room in the back. She came out with a book filled with pictures of the girls.

I was amazed at how beautiful they are. Khadijah was almost a replica of her mother and had her eyes while Angel looked more like me with light brown skin and dark brown eyes. They both had that long, curly, black hair. Flipping through the photo album I got to pictures of them when they were teenagers, and I couldn't believe my eyes. My daughters were beyond beautiful and I wanted to kill myself for missing out on watching them grow. I continued scanning through and came across pictures of the girls with their kids. Angel had a daughter and a son, and Khadijah had a baby boy.

I shut the book and placed it on the glass table in front of me. I looked over at Tracy who's face looked more hurt than pissed and that broke my heart.

"I have to tell you some things."

"Go right ahead."

"Well, I never wanted to mess your life up and I'm truly sorry for everything."

She sat there silently looking over at the wall ignoring me.

"If you and the girls would like to move to California with me, I would be more than happy to take the trip back with you all."

"You got some fuckin' nerve! It's too late for that shit. You should have took us with you when u decided to leave!"

"Well, I'm going to go look for Khadijah and Angel. Do you know where they are right now?"

"They're both at work, but they will all be here this weekend for dinner. Khadijah said she had a surprise for me, whatever that is, but if you would like to come over and see them you can."

"Okay, I will be here."

"It's Sunday and starts at seven."

"Thank you, Tracy."

I got up and hugged her then walked out. Now I was back on the mission to track down my brother's killer.

Khadijah

"A-B-C-D-E-F-G—"

My baby was turning two soon and he was already singing his ABC's clearly; he is so smart. After he was done with the alphabet song, Yatta and I began clapping, making him smile and laugh.

"How old are you going to be Jr.?" Yatta asked him.

He held up two small fingers and to smiled.

"What's that?" I quizzed him.

"Two."

"Alright! Good job, baby."

I watched as he got off our bed and ran into his room. I sat up against the headboard, turned over and looked at Yatta who looked like he had a lot on his mind.

"You okay, baby?"

"Yeah, I'm good. You work today?"

"No, I'm off today. You sure you okay?"

"Honestly, no, I'm not okay."

"Talk to me."

Yatta is my best fucking friend, so when something is bothering him he tells me and vice versa. I love that we can share everything with each other.

"It's like I have too much going on right now in my life, and I just wish I could speak to my mother."

"I can't say it's going to be okay because I don't know what it's like to lose a mother, but baby, I'm here for you and always will be."

We stared at each other for a moment then he lightly grabbed my face and kissed my lips.

"I appreciate you being my side through all this bullshit that's been going on."

"It's no problem, baby."

"I want babies with you, Dijah. I want you to carry my children so they can see that their mother and father love each other, something I never had. Jr. reminds me so much of myself when I was his age, I was a mama's boy."

After hearing him say all that, my ass started crying.

"What's wrong, baby?"

"I want your babies, too, but Yatta I feel you have enough on the way. I don't want to go through a lonely ass pregnancy again."

"What you mean by lonely?"

"Like I did with Jr. What I'm saying is right now you have one baby mama, possibly two, and one is pregnant with twins. You are going to have to be there for them both and me being pregnant would just make shit difficult."

"I'm going to always make that time for you. You are my woman and soon to be wife, so you will never be alone Dijah."

"Soon to be wife?"

"Hell yeah, I'm not letting you go. You are my blessing, of course you wifey."

"Yeah, okay, Yatta."

"You think I'm playing but I'm dead ass serious. You will see."

"You free Sunday night?"

"Yeah, why?"

"I want you to come to dinner with me at my mother's house. My sister's going to be there with her kids too, that way you can meet my family."

"Okay, I got you, baby."

I smiled and got up to do my morning hygiene then did the same for Jr. before I went to the kitchen and began to make breakfast. I loved the fact I have a man who truly cares and loves me and my son. The Most High has really blessed me.

Mary

I hadn't been in contact with Chris in a few days and when I got on Facebook I saw RIP post everywhere. It fucked me up on the inside because I really had feelings for him. If only he had listened to me.

"What you staring off about?"

My friend, Unique asked me.

"Shit, it's just crazy that he gone."

"Yeah, but I'm gone need you to focus on this plan in order to take Yatta out."

"I don't even want to go through with it. That's my cousin's man."

"Don't you want him dead after he killed Chris? You know the police ain't gone do a damn thing about it because he paid they ass good money to keep quiet."

I watched her sit in the chair in front of me rubbing her belly.

"I'm down."

I met Unique at a candlelight that was held for Chris. She was so curious as to who I was and why was I there. I guess she was intimated by me.

"Okay, I'm going to need you to fuck him and get close to him. If he gives you the side bitch position, you take that and use it very well. Once you get close enough you're going to bring him here to your place and get him to tell you about his money and shit, then kill his ass. As for Khadijah, that bitch has to die right along with her nugget head ass son."

"You taking it to fuckin' far, those are still my cousins."

"Look bitch, you can't halfway do the shit. It has to be done in that order."

I turned and looked outside my window and thought of how to go through with the first part of the plan but not killing my cousins.

"Why you so hot with Khadijah, anyway?"

"Because that bitch thinks she's going to play house with my fiancé."

"You told me y'all been broke up though."

I must have struck a nerve because she turned to me with her devilish eyes piercing into mine.

"It doesn't matter, he's mine and she's in the way."

"So why would you kill him if he's yours?"

"Because he killed Chris, now are there anymore fuckin' questions?"

"Not at all."

I shook my head and thought to myself, *this bitch is crazy*. After sitting in an awkward silence for a few minutes, I stood up and went over to my closet.

"Well, I gotta be up out of here by two, so I will meet up with you another time," I said to her as I placed an outfit on my bed.

"Okay, don't back out of this plan just because that's your family. Shit, you think she would hesitate to kill you?"

After she said that, she walked out of my room and I followed her to the door. I opened it, and she walked out but then stopped and turned around.

"I'll be speaking with you again soon."

She had a smirk on her face as she flipped her weave then started walking away. I closed and locked my door then put my Brazilian wave weave into a ponytail before I put a cap over it and started my shower.

When I got in, my head was everywhere and I just broke down. I have never been put in a position like this. I mean, me and Khadijah weren't on the best terms but the bottom line is we share the same blood. I don't think I can go through with this plan, so I made a note to avoid that crazy bitch.

Chapter Sixteen

Tonya

While I was doing hair at my booth, in walked the pregnant chick Khadijah got into it with at the club. I turned to Khadijah and she just continued to do hair, paying the woman no attention.

"What's up, Unique, how could I help you today?" Keisha asked her.

"I want to speak with someone."

I took a look at her hand rubbing her bulging stomach and my heart began to hurt. The fact that she could be carrying Chris's babies pissed me off all over again.

"Speak with who?"

"Khadijah."

Everyone heard her so I turned to Khadijah again, and she just continued to ignore her.

"Well Khadijah is busy right now, so you will have to take this up another time."

I watched as Unique had a smirk on her face.

"Keisha, I know you knew her and Yatta was fucking around so why haven't you told me about that."

"Not my job, you not coming in here with this bullshit. Goodbye."

Keisha pointed her to the door and she turned around and shot a stare at me. I mugged the shit out of her ass; she was so lucky I'm at work.

When she walked out, I saw her walk over to the barbershop. I guess to go see Kenyatta. After I was finished with my client's head, I gave her a mirror so she could examine it then she paid me my money. Khadijah was through with her client's head, so she just sat in her chair scrolling through her phone.

"You okay, Dijah?"

"Yeah, I guess, you could say that."

"What the fuck was that all about?"

She finally looked up at me and shrugged her shoulders. I could tell something was wrong with her.

"I will beat that bitch ass if you want me to. You know I don't give a fuck about her being pregnant," I said in a serious tone and she cracked a smile which made me smile.

"You want to go grab some lunch?" I asked her.

"Yeah, come on."

I grabbed my purse and walked out with her. When we made it to Khadijah's car, there was Yatta and Unique talking. Unique was up in his face and he didn't look like it was a problem, it seemed to me like they ass were caking. Khadijah walked over to them and I was right behind her. They were so engrossed with their conversation that Yatta ain't even notice Khadijah was looking at him.

"So what the fuck is this, Yatta?"

He pushed Unique to the side and she rolled her eyes.

"Nothing, baby."

"It didn't look like nothing when I walked over here."

"Bitch, I told you he's mine and always will be. So go on about your day and have a good one."

"Watch yo' motherfuckin' mouth for real. You know ain't shit going on between us."

"You always play this game Yatta. Tell her you're going to be with me when the twins are—"

Before Unique could finish her sentence, Khadijah punched her right in the mouth, causing her to stumble back holding her leaking lip.

"Call me another bitch and you can have a free abortion. I'm not fucking playing with you, hoe."

Khadijah walked off to her car, and I took one last look at Unique while she held her bleeding lip watching Yatta run after Dijah. When she looked over at me I began to smile because the look on her face was priceless.

"What the fuck you looking at?"

"Yo' hoe ass."

"Who the fuck you calling a hoe? You better watch that shit because I'm not the one."

I chuckled then looked over at Yatta and Dijah talk, but he was hugging on her and she was trying to get him off.

"I know you was fucking with my man Chris, I found the ultrasound at his place. The funny part is you was supposed to be Yatta's bitch, but you fucked one of his guys and got pregnant. You a pathetic ass hoe. Don't think for a second that Yatta is leaving my girl to get back with yo' trifling ass. Dijah is an upgrade, don't you think?"

I nodded my head in the direction of him and Khadijah kissing and that pissed her off, so she stormed off while holding her lip and I laughed. It's a shame how women like her can do that type of shit and think it's cool to walk around like ain't shit wrong. I walked over to my girl and Yatta was walking off. She was cheesing her ass off.

"What's up, Tee, how you doing today?"

"I'm good, bro, thanks for asking."

"No problem, sis."

Yatta walked back into the shop and I hopped into Khadijah's car so we could go get something to eat, finally.

Yatta

When I walked back into the shop, I shook my head at how crazy Dijah's ass been acting lately. Tonight was the night I get to meet her mother and I prayed she wasn't judgmental. After everything that's happened recently in my life, I wish I could hear my mother's voice and see her smiling. I wish I could talk to her about my problems.

My mother was like my life saver. Every time my pops would come home drunk, he would test me by punching me in my chest saying that's how I'd become a man. My mom would always get on him about that shit then he would start hitting her. At the age of three that shit was painful to watch and it never lessened throughout the years. One day, a month before my mother, I was in my room and my dad came home drunk as usual and beat on my mother bad. I was so angry; I waited 'til he was sleep and took his gun from his drawer. I aimed it at him but my mother stopped me. Ever since that night I wished I would have killed his ass. Hearing my phone ringing snapped me out of my thoughts.

"What do you want, Gabby?"

"I miss you, when you coming back?"

"I already told you I'm not coming to see you. Don't call me if it ain't got shit to do with my unborn, I have a girl and I'm not interested in you."

"Well, I lied about being pregnant. I just wanted to see what you were going to do and since that couldn't get you to stay with me, then you can come visit again and we make one for real. I won't tell nobody."

"Is you stupid? I'm glad you not carrying my seed, now bitch stop calling my phone period. I don't want shit to do with you!"

"But Yat—"

Before she could say anything else, I hung up the phone. I blocked her number so she couldn't call me back either. Since she wasn't pregnant, it was no purpose of having any contact with her ass. I couldn't wait to tell Khadijah this. Now the only thing I have to worry about is Unique's ass. Soon as she has those twins I'm getting that DNA test. I placed my phone in my pocket then finished my work for the day.

Khadijah

After getting off of work, I drove over to Angel's crib to pick up my baby. Getting out the car, I walked to her doorstep and knocked on the door. A few seconds later she opened the door with Jr. in her arms. I walked inside and closed her door then headed to the living room.

"Where the kids at?"

"They gone with their daddy. He dropping them off at mama's house, so you should let me ride with you."

"I got something I want to tell you, and it's a surprise for mama."

"What is it?" she asked as she handed me Jr.

I sat on her couch and he laid his head on me.

"I been seeing this guy," I said as I began blushing and Angel began to smile while sitting across from me.

"For how long?"

"About six months now."

Angel's dramatic ass put her hands over her mouth then began smiling.

"My little sister been in a relationship and didn't tell me!"

We both began laughing.

"So who's the lucky guy? Spill everything."

"His name is Yatta and we have a own house out in the suburbs. I love him, that's my baby!"

I blushed at the thought of Yatta and I; I genuinely love that man. He's everything I been looking for, besides his baby mamas and the kids on the way. I never loved anyone besides my son's father, but that was puppy love because this feeling that I have for Yatta defines a whole different kind of love.

"I'm happy for you sister! So he's coming to dinner tonight?"

"Yeah, that's the surprise ma doesn't know about."

"That name is familiar though. What does he do?"

"He's a barber, he has his own shop," I said not wanting to tell her his side business.

"Ah snap, okay, I see y'all. Why you wait so long to tell me? I mean, we tell each other everything."

"It's a long story, but I just wanted to make sure we were on the same page, that's all."

144

"Well I can't wait to meet him."

Looking at my iPhone 6 Plus, I saw Yatta sent me a text telling me he made it to the house and was about to get dressed. I responded back and told him I was on my way.

"So you getting dressed at my place?" I asked my sister.

"Yeah, my clothes already in the bag, I'm ready."

"Okay, and you said the kids gone be dropped off at mom's, right?"

"Yeah."

"Okay, come on."

I watched her grab her keys, purse and her bag then locked up. After locking Jr. in his car seat, I got in and angel sat in the passenger seat as we headed to my house.

After the hour drive, I finally arrived to the house and parked my car on the side of Yatta's in our circular drive way.

"Oh my fuckin' God, Dijah! This place looks huge!" Angel said as she closed the door then went to the trunk to get her things.

I went round the car to get my baby out his seat and carried him up the steps. After I unlocked the door and stepped aside for Angel to enter, she placed her hand over her heart and looked like she was about to faint. I smiled at her and imagined I must have had the same reaction the day we moved in.

"Baby, I'm home!"

"Dijah, why you been holding out?"

"I haven't, we just moved in here not too long ago."

145

I knew she was amazed by our place. The floors were waxed and sparkling, the dining room was nice and neat, and the décor was immaculate. Yatta came down the stairs in a black, Polo suit with black, dress shoes and his hair braided back neatly, letting his dreads fall down to the middle of his back. His tall, fine ass walked over to me and my stomach began to get butterflies like I had just met him.

We kissed then he looked at Angel, so I cleared my throat.

"Baby, this is my big sister, Angel. She's the only sibling I have, actually, and Angel this is Kenyatta."

I watched the two exchange smiles and shake each other's hands.

"It's nice to finally meet you, Yatta."

"And it's a pleasure meeting you. Y'all asses look just alike. If it wasn't for y'all having different complexions y'all could pass as twins."

"I'm always told I look like my father, but me and Dijah are starting to look alike."

I shook my head then put Jr. on the couch and he woke up.

"Hey daddy!"

He jumped up running over to Yatta. Yatta caught him and held him in the air, tickling him before they hugged.

"What's up, lil man?"

"Where you going?"

"I'm going to grandma's tonight."

"I want to go too!"

"You going soon as soon as you get dressed," Yatta told him, "Dijah I'm about to go get him dressed so you can get yourself together."

146

"Okay, thanks, baby."

I watched as Yatta held Jr. and walked upstairs, listening to him talk his ears off.

"Aww, that's so sweet. I can't believe he's calling him daddy and all."

"Yes, it shocked the hell out of me when he first called him that. Their bond is like they are real blood. It's crazy because I always wished for Kenny to get his shit together so he could be a good father to Jr., but I guess he just ain't want to. Not to mention he's trying to take me to court to get full custody of him."

"You serious?"

"Hell yeah, he talking about I never let him come and get Jr. or let him go see his grandmother. But what I was trying to explain to him was Jr. doesn't even know any of them, none of them motherfuckers came to see how he was doing or see if he needed anything. Now all of a sudden motherfuckers want to see him? Girl, they ass a damn trip right along with Kenny deadbeat ass."

"Calm down, Dijah, damn. But they ass really tripping, especially Kenny. Full custody? That man is crazy."

"I get pissed off every time I think about that shit."

"Where the bathroom and spare room so I can get dressed?"

"The bathroom is down this hall to the right and it's a bedroom right across from it."

I watched as Angel passed the kitchen, touching the granite countertops then walked down the hall. I went upstairs to my bedroom to pick out something to wear. After I showered, I applied body oil on from head to toe then slipped on my black, sleeveless, bodycon dress with a pair of silver red bottoms. I took the shower cap off first then removed my bonnet and combed my hair out. It was bone straight, so all

I had to do was spray it with some olive oil sheen. After I put in my diamond stud earrings, I looked at myself in the mirror and as soon as I was about to turn away Yatta walked in.

"You nervous?"

"Hell yeah."

"Don't be, baby. My mom is not judgmental or ignorant."

I watched him as he sat down on the bed, then put his head in his hands so I sat next to him.

"It's going to be okay, baby."

I kissed his neck, then his ear, and up to his cheek before he turned to me and kissed me on the lips with so much passion.

"You look beautiful. Jr.'s ready."

A few seconds later Jr. walked in dressed just like Yatta and it was so cute.

"Mommy, you like my suit daddy put on me? I'm dressed just like him."

"You look handsome, baby. Both you and daddy are handsome in your suits."

He ran over to me giving me the biggest hug ever, and these are the moments I loved.

Chapter Seventeen

Yatta

Driving over to Khadijah's mother's house wasn't that long because she was only about 25 minutes away from us. When we arrived, I grabbed little man and carried him as Dijah and Angel walked up to the door, ringing the bell. It was kind of chilly outside, so I prayed she didn't take all day opening the door.

"Hey, my babies!" she yelled as soon as she opened the door and hugged Dijah and Angel. Then she looked at me and back at her girls.

"Come on in."

We all walked in and I put Jr. down. He took off his coat and I did the same.

"Now, who's man is this?" their mother asked, looking back and forth between Dijah and her sister.

"He's mine," Dijah spoke up.

"How long you two been dating?"

"Six months now," I said causing her to look over at me.
Her eyes were light green and her long, brown hair was up in a bun. Dijah's mother may be white, but her spirit and vibe was like a black person's.

"Well, it's nice meeting you. My name is Tracy, what's yours?"

"Kenyatta, and its nice meeting you as well."

I reached my hand out for her to shake it, but instead she looked at me like I had three heads on my shoulder. She reached in for a hug and I hugged her back. She was the same height as Dijah, short but they were all built alike and that was thick.

"Heyyy, granny man."

She turned to Jr. and picked him up and he hugged her tight.

"Where are my other grandchildren?"

"Their daddy's dropping them off here a little bit later."

"Okay, you guys can get comfortable while I finishing cooking this meal. Yatta I have beers in the refrigerator if you drink those, the remote is on top of the TV right there."

"Okay."

I sat on the cream colored couch and Dijah passed me the remote. After she kissed me, she headed in the same direction as her mother Little man came and sat on the couch by me and laid his head on my arm, so I lifted my arm and put it on the back of the sofa so he could lay against me. Dijah walked back in and handed me a beer and I began to drink it as I flicked through channels. Smelling the aroma of the dinner had my stomach growling.

Khadijah

I walked back into the kitchen with my mother and Angel and they were talking about special guest.

"What special guest? You been dating, ma?"

"Of course not, girl I'm not looking for no relationship at this age. I been focused on keeping my health good and that's all."

"Mhm, so who's the special guest then?" I asked looking at her while she checked on the baked chicken. I could see it was covered in green peppers and onions. It smelled so good you could tell it was well-seasoned.

"A surprise for you all."

I looked over at Angel and we both looked confused, but we helped her finish preparing the macaroni and cheese, sweet potatoes, greens, cornbread, and an apple pie along with chocolate cake.

After everything was almost done, the doorbell rung and I went to answer the door.

"Who is it?"

"Ken."

When I heard that name and that voice, my heart dropped down to the pit of my stomach and I froze. After hearing the doorbell again, Yatta got up and asked who was it. He repeated his name and when Yatta opened the door, I was face to face with my daddy. After of the years he's been gone, he thought it was cool to just pop up at mama's house? Once he stepped in, Yatta closed the door then looked over at me.

"Who was at the door?" Angel asked. She paused in her tracks looking at daddy and mama came right behind her.

"Well, this was my surprise, so surprise!"

The room was silent and Yatta was looking confused.

"You ladies are beautiful. I know I've missed out on so much, but right now I just want to ask you two to forgive me. I want a chance to get to know y'all," he finally spoke up.

"Why did you leave us?" I asked.

"I had a lot going on here, so I had to leave right away."

"You couldn't take us with you?" Angel asked.

"I could have, but I wasn't thinking. I was young and was mixed up in a lot different shit."

I walked over to the couch and sat next to my sleeping son. I was furious right now. His excuse for why he missed out on so much because he was young sounded just like Kenny and that pissed me the fuck off.

"Who is this?" He asked, pointing to Yatta.

"My man," I said with an attitude.

"What's your name?"

"Kenyatta."

"Well I'm Ken, Khadijah's father."

"Nice meeting you, sir."

They shook hands before he turned to Angel.

"Where's the rest of my grandkids?"

"They should be here any second now."

Just when Angel said it the doorbell rung and there were my niece and nephew. My niece and nephew were a year apart and they were my heart as much as Jr. was. Terry was three years old and Trina was two. They ran and hugged their grandmother then came and hugged me. I looked over at my father and he was admiring them; I could see sorrow in his eyes.

"Come here," Angel said to them and they both walked over to her.

"This is your grandpa."

They both looked at him then gave him a hug. That made me smile on the inside. Angel walked off wiping tears from her face. It made me get a little emotional, but I didn't let a tear fall. The rest of the night went well. The kids ate and played with each other while my mom, dad, Angel, Kenyatta and I talked.

It was now ten-thirty in the evening and we were on the way home. We said our goodbyes to everyone, including Angel because she was waiting on her children's father to come and get them. After arriving home, I gave Jr. a bath then put on his night clothes. I tucked him in and read him a bedtime story as he drifted to sleep. Turning his night light on, I kissed his forehead then closed his door. Walking into my bedroom I saw Yatta laying on the bed with his suit still on.

"Baby, you want to come shower with me?"

He jumped up quick as hell and I laughed at him while he rushed to undo his tie and unbutton his shirt. I went into our walk-in bathroom and ran warm water for our shower before I got undressed. We both got in and the water hit us from every angle causing our hair to get wet.

"I love you baby," he said to me while pulling me close to him.

"I love you more."

We shared an electrifying kiss before he got on his knees and started to devour my box. Grabbing his head, I tried to pull him away but that only caused him to suck harder on my pearl which made me yell out in pleasure. Feeling my legs began to shake, he got up, put my leg down, bent me over and slid right inside of me.

"Ohhh my God!" I screamed while my hands were on the sky blue tiles in the shower.

Feeling him go in and out of me with so much force caused a rush throughout my body which made me have a big ass climax and he came right after me. I turned around and we stared at each other in silence. He grabbed my washcloth and put Caress body wash on it and began to wash me up. After I rinsed the soap off me I grabbed his washcloth, poured his Old Spice *Swagger* body wash on it and returned the favor. After we were done with our shower, we dried off and put our night clothes on and got in bed.

Hearing Yatta's phone go off right before we were about to drift off frustrated me.

"Hello?"

I couldn't make out who was on the other line, but I think it was his homeboy Jay. After a few more seconds on the phone, I heard him say he would be on his way and I rolled my eyes as he hung the phone up.

"Baby, that was Jay. He wanted to meet up with me to discuss some shit that just happened at the trap. Don't wait up for me because I don't want you to be tired in the morning."

"What happened?"

"He said it almost caught on fire, but he got there in time to put it out. I'm gone handle this real quick and see you soon."

He walked over to me after getting dressed and gave me a quick kiss on the lips. I laid back down as he exited the bedroom and out the house.

Kenyatta

"Who was the last person at the trap?"

"Last one there for lock up was Boo."

Boo was another young nigga and he's been working for me for a couple of years now. He was in his senior year of school, but I hit him up not caring that it was now one in the morning.

"Yo," he said into the phone sounding like he was still asleep.

"Meet me at the spot now, and don't take all day."

"A'ight."

I hung the phone up and put it on the table. After inspecting everything in the trap, I didn't see anything out of the ordinary.

"Nigga yo' ass been MIA for a minute. You being a family man, playing house and shit."

"Yeah, that's my baby. She's wifey."

"How you turn soft to a stripper? Damn near the whole hood seen her body naked, nigga."

"That don't mean shit to me. She had to do what she had to do, that was her past."

"I guess."

"Yo' ass just mad because you couldn't cuff."

He rubbed his hands together with a smile on his face.

"You damn right nigga, she bad as fuck. She would look better if she was on my arm," he said playfully causing us both to laugh.

Just when I was about to say something else, Boo walked in looking half sleep.

"What's up man, it's damn near two in the morning. You know I got school?"

"You almost let the trap burn down."

He scrunched his face up then sat in the seat across from me.

"I didn't let shit almost get burned down."

"You was the last person to lock up. I came just in time before the flames spread, it was in the back," Jay said.

"So what the fuck were you doing before you left?"

"I was making sure everything was in place and yo' chick that's pregnant came by. I think she said her name was Unique. She said you told her she could come by and get some shit out your office upstairs. I made sure she left before I locked up."

"What the fuck she leave out with?" I asked him standing up, heading up to my office.

"I didn't see her leave out with nothing, she didn't even have a purse on her. She probably went to the back and grabbed that gas and lit that shit. I didn't do the shit."

"I'm not messing with that bitch no more, and how the fuck she found out where the fuck my trap at in the first fucking place!"

When I got to my office, I checked every last one of my stashes and they were untouched as I expected because her ass didn't know none of the codes. I went back down stairs and stood in front of Boo.

"Look, don't let that bitch come in here again. I don't fuck with her, that bitch a snake. Make sure you tell everybody else that. I'm gone have another meeting."

"A'ight I got you, boss."

I watched as Boo walked out the trap and looked over at Jay who had a confused look on his face.

"Somebody must have told her ass about this trap and only the guys know bro."

"I'm about to go pay that bitch a visit, make sure u lock this shit up."

"A'ight."

Chapter Eighteen

Unique

After getting out of the shower, I was exhausted. Thank God Tasha finally got a bed in her second bedroom and just in time because my stomach was getting bigger every day. I could not fit on that couch anymore let alone get comfortable. As soon as I laid down, I heard a car pull up and then banging at the door. Since Tasha was out for the night with her bae, I knew I was going to have to see who it was because they wouldn't let up on the banging.

Looking at the time on my phone I saw that it was after two in the morning. That didn't stop whoever was at the door though because the banging grew louder. Looking through the peephole I saw it was Yatta, and by the look on his face I could tell it wasn't good.

"Open up this fuckin' door!"

As soon as the knob twisted, he pushed passed me and slammed the door. He grabbed me by both of my arms so tight that I could feel my blood circulation being cut off.

"Why the fuck you try to burn down my damn trap? You know that's how I make the most fuckin' money!"

"I don't even know nothing about your traps. Now can you let me go? You're hurting me."

"You a fuckin' lie. Boo said he let you in before he locked up, so what the fuck you take out of my office?"

He squeezed my arms more causing me to wince out in pain, but he didn't care. He had this dark look in his eyes. This was not the Yatta I knew.

"I didn't take anything, Yatta, I swear. I'm sorry, just let me go please, you're hurting me!"

He let go of my arms causing me to rub them. They felt sore and there was a burning sensation where his hands were.

"So how the fuck you find where my trap was?"

"Somebody told me."

I could see that answer pissed him off because he rushed over to me, pushed me up against the wall and began to choke me.

"Bitch, I'm not playing with you. I'm dead fucking serious, stay the fuck away from my motherfuckin' trap. If I catch yo' ass around there or hear about you coming around there, I will fuckin' kill you, bitch. Do you understand me!"

I couldn't breathe. I tried to pry his hands from around my neck but before I could he slapped the shit out of me and dropped me to the floor. As I laid down on the floor, gasping for air, he yanked me by my hair so I could look him in the eyes.

"I said, do you fuckin' understand me?"

I waited for a second to catch my breath.

"Yes, I understand Yatta."

He threw my head back and walked out, slamming the door behind him. Tears instantly ran down my face at how he just chocked me and hit me. Never had he done any that to me. I guess I deserved it because I did try to burn his trap down, but I'm pregnant and he had no fucking right to put his hands on me.

I went back up to my room and balled up as much as I could and cried. My feelings were hurt and I could not believe this was my life right now. Sleeping with Chris behind Yatta's back wasn't right, but he should understand that I still love him. The only reason I'm acting out is because I don't know how to get him to see that I still want to be with him; I want us to be a family like we always talked about. I cried and cried until I fell asleep.

Tonya

Running to the bathroom to throw up for the third time today was overrated. After I washed my hands and rinsed my mouth, I walked out of the bathroom. Keshia and Khadijah kept giving me questioning stares, but I just ignored them. I know what they were thinking and that was not it.

"What you getting today?" I asked my customer with a smile.

"I want those Marley twist, but a medium size."

"Okay, I got you, what colors you want?"

"Just all black."

"Okay."

As I began taking the hair out the pack, the nauseous feeling came over me again causing me to run to the back again. This time it was clear and my stomach felt so empty while my throat hurt from the constant vomiting. Feeling weak, I flushed and came out the stall to see Khadijah standing by the sink. I washed my hands then began rinsing my mouth out before I grabbed a paper towel. I placed my hands on the sink as I put my head down and cried.

Feeling Khadijah rub my back helped me feel a little better, but not much.

"You want to go down to the clinic on break?"

"We could, but I'm scared."

"When was your last period?"

I thought back and realized I haven't had a period in over five months, but I really wasn't expecting to be pregnant because I had been taking my pills regularly. I haven't had any signs of pregnancy at all so I don't see how it could be a possibility.

"Like five months."

"Are you serious?"

"Yes, I thought nothing of it because I've been taking my pills."

"Not for five months, Tee."

I began crying and Dijah pulled me into her arms as I sobbed on her shoulder.

"I can't be pregnant Dijah, my baby won't have a father!"

"Ok look, we are going to go down to the clinic soon as we go on break. We will get this figured out, okay? I'm here for you no matter what."

The words coming out of Dijah's mouth were soothing to me, but in reality I was still hurt at the fact I could be pregnant and didn't know it. What if my baby comes out deformed because I continued taking the pills? What's worse is my baby won't have a father because he's dead. I had a lot on my mind and it was hard not to think about it, but I put it all behind me. I went back to work, making sure I had my water bottle with me.

When I finished, my client paid me and I walked to the back throwing away my empty water bottle. I grabbed another and walked back up to the front. I sat in my chair waiting for Dijah to get done with her client's hair.

By the time Dijah was finished, Yatta and some guy walked in. I'm not even gonna stunt, I've seen him hanging with Chris before but Chris didn't really like me hanging with him and his boys. Therefore, I never really got the chance to converse and chill with any of them.

"What's up sis? How you feeling today?" Yatta asked me.

"I'm good bro."

He gave me a head nod before walking to the back with Dijah. Looking at the man that walked in with him was getting me hot. The way his jewelry shined against the light had me lost for words and his weaves had me ready to go back to the bathroom, but I controlled myself as he walked over to me.

"How you doing, lady?"

"I umm… I'm good."

He got closer and his caramel skin, along with his tall frame and muscular body had me ready to scream and take him down right in this shop.

"I've seen you before, weren't you Chris's girl?"

"Yeah."

"I'm sorry for your lost, what's your name again?"

"Tonya."

"I'm Jay."

He reached his hand out for me to shake it and I did. Keshia walked up and spoke to Jay, saving me the embarrassment of looking clueless.

"What's up Jay, what's been going on?"

"Shit, just been taking it day by day, you know? What been up with you?"

"Making this money and staying out of trouble."

"True, nothing wrong with that."

When Keshia walked out of the salon, Jay's sexy brown eyes were back on me. He was smiling showing off his perfect, pearly whites.

"So how you been doing Tonya?"

"I've been ok."

I felt my palms getting sweaty so I rubbed them onto my black pants I was wearing.

"Well it was nice seeing you Tonya, take care."

The stare he gave me had me on cloud nine. This man here had me ready to do a whole lot of freaky shit to him. I was so lost in my thoughts I didn't even notice Khadijah was standing right next to me. As I watched Jay leave out with Yatta, he never took his eyes off mine.

"Mhm, I see that shit."

"See what? I don't know what you talking about."

"Girl I'm not stupid, I saw you and Jay making eyes and shit. You ready?"

A grin came across my face as I began to get a feeling inside that I wasn't sure if I was supposed to be feeling just yet.

"Yeah I'm ready, but Keshia went to the store real quick."

"Okay, we can wait till she gets back. How you feeling now?"

"I feel okay. Hungry now, but I'm still not understanding how could I be pregnant and not have any symptoms till now. My stomach not even showing."

"Females with flat stomachs don't really start showing until the beginning of their last trimester. so that explains the stomach part. As far as symptoms, was Chris acting funny around you, like throwing up, weird eating habits, or anything? Because they say when the female doesn't get the symptoms the man does."

"I've seen him throwing up a couple of times but I thought it was from him having hangovers. I did see him eating pickles with peanut butter, but never really questioned him about it. Damn Dijah, I can't do this."

My emotions got the best of me. Missing the hell out of Chris and the possibility of me being pregnant wasn't making me feel any better. Tears began running down my face and I just sat in a blank stare feeling numb, hurt, and mad at the same time.

"I really hate seeing you like this. If I could bring Chris back I would, even though his cheating ass ain't shit, but for you I would bring him back. This pain I see you going through is not right at all."

Dijah was right, I was all over the place and I had to remind myself to get it together while I was at work. So I made a note in my head to take a few days off because emotionally, I just couldn't be here. Keisha walked in with a smile, but it faded as soon as she seen my face.

"Damn I only left for thirty seconds and I come back you crying. What's going on?"

I looked at Dijah signaling for her to tell Keisha because at the moment the lump in my throat wouldn't let me speak.

"She's going through a lot right now."

"Well baby whatever it is it will get better. The Most High always has you under his wing, he wouldn't put nothing on you that you couldn't handle. It will be okay, baby girl. Remember, He gives His toughest troubles to His strongest soldiers."

Keshia saying those words to me and rubbing my back before walking to the back was all I needed to hear. Wiping the tears from my face, I got up and packed everything I needed inside my Gucci purse and Khadijah did the same.

"Aye Keshia, our break probably gone be a little bit longer today!"

Keisha walked back to the front.

"It's okay, y'all don't have any more clients lined up for today?"

I shook my head and Dijah said no.

"Okay, I will just close up early. Y'all take care and see y'all Monday."

"Okay, bye Keisha," Dijah said.

"Bye Keisha," I said.

"You take care Tonya. If you need time off just let me know, okay?"

"Okay."

After walking out, Dijah and I got in our cars and I followed her to the clinic which was just four blocks down from the salon. Getting out, we both walked inside. Surprisingly, it wasn't crowded and that was a blessing.

"May I help you?" a brown skin, thick lady said from behind the counter.

"Yes, I'm here for the free pregnancy test."

"Okay, fill out this form and I will be right with you."

I took the clipboard she passed to me before sitting in the closet chair to counter and Dijah sat next to me. I was happy she wasn't leaving my side in my time of need.

After I finished the paperwork, I returned it to the receptionist and in return she handed me a urine cup. I left my purse and phone with Dijah as I walked to the bathroom. It felt like forever before I finally reached it and twisted the knob; I closed the door and locked it, twisted the cap off the cup, and began to pull my pants. A few seconds passed before I felt the urge to pee but once it hit, I urinated inside the cup and filled it to the brim.

After I was done, I put the cup on the floor in front of me and carefully screwed the top back on. I then wiped myself and flushed the toilet. Before washing my hands I grabbed a few paper towels and wiped the cup down, then put plenty of soap in my hands, thoroughly clean them. I dried my hands as I bent over to pick up the cup, then threw the paper away and walked out. Putting the cup onto the side of the counter, I sat down next to Dijah and watched the receptionist put on a pair clear gloves and took the cup to the back.

I laid on Dijah's shoulder and she caressed my head. Five minutes later, the lady came back to the desk and told me to come to the back with her. As I entered the room she sat at a desk and I sat across from her. She placed some paper towels on a small metal table beside her and placed a pregnancy test down before she opened my urine sample and dipped the pregnancy test in it. She laid it flat on the table and waited for the results as I sat in silence, staring at my hands the whole time.

When the time went off, she read the test then showed me and the results and it was positive. After she cleaned the area where she did the pregnancy test, she came and sat back in front of me and went through my paper work.

"According to your last period, you're about eighteen weeks now."

My heart sunk deep down into my stomach from hearing her say that. Watching her get back up grabbing some papers about pregnancy, she handed them to me and I thanked her as I walked out. Dijah could read the answer from my facial expression, so she just opened her arms as she cried with me. After about two minutes, we got ourselves together and grabbed our things to leave.

"She told me I'm about eighteen weeks."

"It's going to be okay, my niece or nephew is going to be straight. We got this, okay?"

"Okay."

Just when I was about to walk to my car Dijah called out to me.

"Aye, you want to come stay at my place?"

"I don't want to be in your place, you and Yatta need y'all time alone."

"Well I know you haven't been to your house and I'm positive you really don't want to go back to your moms' house, so just come stay with me. Yatta won't mind."

"Okay, thank you so much."

"It's no problem Tee."

We both got inside of our cars and rode all the way to Dijah's place. The whole way there it felt like the radio knew my mood because every song they played was sad. I ended up just cutting it off. I couldn't believe my life right now; I just wanted to rest for a couple of days because the recent events plus finding out I'm pregnant was too much for me right now but I heard Keshia's words replay in my head.

He gives his toughest battles to his strongest soldiers.

Kenyatta

"Man I don't think you want to talk to her, she's still mourning the death of Chris."

"I don't give a damn, shit that's even more reason to talk to her."

"Don't be on no playa type shit with her, that's sis."

168

"I already know."

Walking to the front of the shop, I sat in my chair waiting for my client to arrive and in walked Kenny's bitch ass.

"Why the fuck are you here?" I asked.

"I came to get lined up and have a talk with you."

I got up from the chair staring him down before moving to the side so he could sit in my chair. Jay stood in front of him as he sat down.

"What the fuck you looking at nigga?"

Jay reached in the small of his back for his gun, but I stopped him.

"Jay man it's cool, you know I don't want shit happening in this shop."

"A'ight bet."

Jay walked out and left as I wrapped the cap around Kenny and began to clean my clippers.

"So how you like playing daddy to my son?"

I wiped down the clippers one more time before cutting them on and started to use them.

"It's great, he's a smart young man. He calls you daddy?"

"I haven't seen him for him to call me daddy but that's gone change."

"Why haven't you seen your son since birth, yet now you want custody of him? Why is that?"

"Because that's my motherfuckin' son and that bitch keeping him from me but have you around him. You ain't no fuckin' good influence on him."

"Oh and I'm guessing you're the best influence he needs huh? You don't even know nothing about the boy. Least I take the time out and spend time with him, you can't even come by the house and kick it with him. That's fucked up."

"I don't have to go over there to spend time with him when I can just come pick him up. That bitch can't keep me from my son."

"Watch your mouth bro."

"Don't bro me, Yatta. I know you had something to do with my brother's death and don't think for a second this shit is over. I'm getting and I'm coming for payback nigga. You ain't go have no power on these streets no more."

"Was that a threat? You know I don't do well with those so say what the fuck you trying to say nigga."

Just when he was about to talk I ran the clippers across the back of his neck and he jumped.

"Fuck man!"

Everyone looked over at us as he took the cap off and got up, holding the back of his neck. I knew for a fact that if him and I were to ever fight, I would beat the dog shit out of his skinny ass. This nigga had no muscle to him. We stared each other up and down before he began to speak.

"This shit not over!"

I stood in my stance and just nodded my head at him. If he even thought about killing me, I would know ahead of time because one thing about me is I don't sit around and wait for shit to pop off; I just go kill before it gets out of hand so if the nigga was smart, he would go running out of Chicago.

I chuckled to myself at the fact that this nigga was intimidated by me. It was only a matter of time before they brought out the old Yatta and niggas was gone really feel my pain. Walking out the store I called Dijah to check on her and she answered on the second ring.

"Hey baby."

"What's up sweetheart, what you doing?"

"Just made it back home. I'm going to pick Jr. up a little bit later but I told Tonya she could stay with us for a while because she's going through a lot right now. I'll talk to you about it when you get home."

"Okay that's cool, I'll see you later, you want me to pick up something to eat on my way home?"

"Yeah, because I don't feel like cooking tonight. I'm too tired."

"No problem baby, I got you."

"I love you."

"I love you too, sweetheart."

I hung up the phone as my client walked in and I began to cut his hair. After another hour passed I closed up the shop, made my way to my car and headed over to Margarita's Pizza. Inside I stood in line and waited but from the corner of my eye I could see someone staring at me. I looked over and there was this dark skin chick with thick thighs and a beautiful face.

"Hello," she said with a smile showing off her perfect teeth.

"How you doing?"

"I'm good, what about yourself?"

"I'm straight, just trying to get this pizza and head home."

"Ah ok."

The look on her face was telling me she wanted to say more but I just couldn't pin point it. Once I gave cashier my order, I went out to my car and rolled up a blunt and smoked while I waited. A few minutes into my smoke session. the dark skin shorty walked over to me.

"Can I join?"

I wasn't thinking right so I let her hit the blunt and we began having conversation.

"What's your name?"

"Mary, and I already know yours."

"And how is that?"

"Who doesn't know you, Yatta?"

I began laughing at the fact she was referring to my street status.

"True, you right."

"So how's your love life going?"

"I don't want to talk about that right now."

A smirk crossed her face, but I paid it no mind.

"So when am I gonna see you again?"

"Shit we could go back to my spot if you want."

"What about the pizza?"

"Fuck that pizza," I said.

After I said that, she hoped in her car and waited for me to drive so she could follow behind me. When we arrived to my condo, I parked my car and she did the same before getting out fixing her long weave. Her hips had me mesmerized as she walked over to me and I couldn't help but to grab her from behind as we walked inside. Cutting on the lights I locked my door and sat my phone down on the table. I then went to the kitchen and grabbed some Hennessy.

Pouring our glasses, I walked over to her and handed it to her.

"Ka—"

Stopping myself from calling her Khadijah made me snapped back to reality. I began to drink my cup and sat next to her.

"So where you from?" I asked her.

"I'm from the hundreds."

Looking at her I could tell she was getting drunk, so I went to my room and rolled me up a couple of blunts. As I lit the first one I heard shorty's heels walking towards my room and she came and sat next to me. Paying her no attention, I continued to hit the blunt and she stood up taking her clothes off. Staring at her breast had me ready to take her down, but my phone began ringing.

I saw it was Khadijah, but I put it on silent and laid back on the bed as I continued to smoke. I watched her take off her jeans after she removed her heels, then she walked over to me tugging down my jogging pants. Her eyes got big as she looked at my manhood and I could tell she liked what she was saw.

She began stroking my manhood up and down before taking me in her mouth.

"Fuck!" I groaned as her warm mouth went up and down my shaft making bubbles. The shit felt so good I grabbed her head and pumped in and out of her mouth with force. After coming in her mouth. she stood up and I smacked her on the ass as she made it clap. Going inside my dresser I pulled out a magnum and slid it on my manhood.

"Come ride this dick ma."

She walked over to me, straddled me and put my manhood inside of her. Feeling how tight she was, I raised her thick ass up and took the rubber off so I could feel how wet she was. I stuck my manhood back inside of her causing her to moan loud. After fucking her in the same position for ten minutes, I flipped her over and started hitting her from the back. Her thick ass was throwing it back and I went deeper.

Hearing her moan and feeling her cum on my dick while I continued to dig deep inside her was the best feeling.

"Fuck Yatta, I'm about to cum!"

"Hold that shit!" I said smacking her ass hard on both checks.

She began throwing her ass back harder and she came again. Right before I was about to cum I pulled out. She turned around and took me in her mouth and I came.

Laying back on the bed I pushed my dreads back and began to light another blunt. Passing it to her after taking a few hits, I got up and walked to the bathroom to take a shower. I let the hot water run down my body for a moment before I began washing up. I got out and Khadijah was heavy on my mind. It just dawned on me that I had just cheated on her. Feeling like shit, I got dressed and walked back to the room where Mary's ass was still undressed smoking the last of the blunt.

"Aye, you gotta get out."

"Why? I thought I was spending the night?"

"Naw, I'm about to make some moves so you need to get yo shit on and head out."

I sat on the bed with my hands over my face and she walked over to me touching my back.

"You okay?"

"Yeah, I'm good."

She tried to kiss me when we made eye contact but I moved.

"Why you acting like that then?"

"Because you need to get the fuck out!" I snapped feeling my blood pressure rise. I couldn't get mad at nobody for my stupid ass decisions but my damn self.

"Why you getting loud with me? you didn't have an attitude with me a few minutes ago so I'm trying to figure out what the fuck is your problem."

I looked up at her as she put her clothes and heels back on.

"Just to let you know, I'm not some hoe that you fucked and think you can talk or treat any type of way, Yatta."

"I'm not trying to hear that shit."

"But I bet my cousin will," she smirked then turned to walk out of the bedroom, but I got up and grabbed her arm before she could leave out the door.

"Who the fuck is your cousin?"

"Your girlfriend, Khadijah. Now let me the fuck go you're hurting me."

When she said Khadijah is her cousin, I felt like I was hit with a ton of bricks. I grabbed her by her throat and pinned her up against the wall.

"Who the fuck sent you!"

I wasn't a dumb nigga at all. I could sense from her vibe that something was up, but I took that fucking risk and that's what pissed me off the most. Looking into her eyes and feeling her nails scratching my hand I let her go. She tried to run and leave out the door but didn't succeed because I snatched her by her hair and threw her down to the floor.

"Bitch, answer my question!"

She began to cry as she held on to her neck. I went over to the couch and pulled my gun from up under the cushion and walked back over to her, bending down to her level. Cocking the gun, I aimed it at her head.

"Who the fuck sent you!"

"It was Unique! Unique wanted me to kill you and Dijah!"

With those last words being said, I let off two shots to her head and she dropped lifeless with her eyes opened. I picked up my phone and dialed Jay's number.

"Aye bro, have some clean up niggas come down to my condo."

"A'ight."

I stepped over Mary's lifeless body and grabbed the Hennessy bottle taking a big swig. How the fuck could I be so fucking stupid? I knew something about that bitch wasn't right. Something told me to just go home, but that wouldn't have made any difference because Unique wanted me and the love of my life dead. Eventually, shit was going to hit the fan. I'm just glad ain't shit happen to me or my girl.

I felt myself getting tipsy as I heard a knock at the door, and it was the cleaning crew. After they took her body out, they cleaned my floor of her blood. A few minutes later Jay walked in looking around and then down at the spot they were cleaning.

"What the fuck happen?"

"I fucked up."

"What the fuck happened, Yatta?"

I took a few more sips from the bottle feeling numb.

"I killed Khadijah's cousin."

"What the fuck?"

"That bitch was in on some plan Unique has to kill me and Khadijah. you know I had to kill her bro, it wasn't no way that bitch was walking out of here."

"Unique?"

"Hell yeah bro, this bitch just doing anything but I see how she doing this shit now."

"What you gone do now man?"

"I'm gone kill that bitch next. Soon as she has them babies that bitch is dead."

"Damn man, I can't believe this shit."

"She being a sneaky, spiteful bitch and all this shit is about to stop soon as these four months fly pass."

Jay shook his head then looked at me drinking my bottle.

"I need me to drop you off because you can't be driving all fucked up," he looked around for a second, "Aye, I'll pay you two hundred extra to follow me in his car," he said to one of the men.

He put his cleaning shit down and I handed him my keys and we left. When we arrived to my house, I felt sick as a dog; I didn't even think I could face Khadijah after I just cheated on her.

"It's two in the morning. What the fuck do I tell her man?"

"You tell her you was out catching up on business."

I shook my head not wanting to lie to her, but it was my only option to keep her with me.

"Thanks for the ride bro."

"No problem."

I got out and so did the guy Jay paid to drive my car. He walked to me handing me my keys then got in the car with Jay. They drove off just as I had closed and locked the door.

Not wanting to turn on any lights, I had to carefully make my way upstairs to the bedroom. When I made it, Khadijah was sitting up in bed with her knees pulled up to her chest. As soon as I looked at her I could tell she had been crying.

"What's wrong Dijah?"

"So who is she Yatta."

I sighed and sat down holding my head down with my back turned towards her.

"You coming in here at two in the morning smelling like liquor, so who is she I'm not dumb."

Her voice cracked then she began to sob. My silence spoke volumes. I felt her get up and she walked over to me. I couldn't even look at her so I kept my head down.

"Why the fuck do I have to go through this shit, huh? I thought you weren't going to hurt me Ya. Why? Why you doing this to me?"

When I still didn't answer her, she began punching me in the head, arms, and chest. I got up and grabbed her, then hugged her and she just stood in my arms crying. I hated I was the cause of her pain, it hurt me on the inside. I felt her break away from the hug and she looked at me with tears in her now grey eyes.

"I'm leaving."

"What you mean you leaving?"

"I'm leaving you Yatta, I can't be with you. You only care about yourself and just want to be alone."

When she said that, she grabbed her already packed suitcases that I didn't even notice. She began walking out the room and I followed behind her.

"You can't just leave me like this Dijah! It's two in the morning, where you going? You can't wake Jr. up out his sleep."

"I never went and got him from Angels and Tonya left to go to her mom's. I'm leaving away from you so don't worry about where I'm going."

She walked down the stairs, and I'm not gone lie, seeing her walk away from me with them suitcases hurt me to death. Before she could unlock the door, I stopped her and held her hands causing her to look up at me with tears still falling from her eyes.

"Look baby, I promise whatever you want me to do I will. Just please don't leave me, I need you right now."

"You should have thought about that before you cheated on me Yatta. I'm not about to sit around and let you do what you want, no, I'm not going to let it happen!"

What she was saying in between her sobs was true. It was my choice to cheat on her; I made that decision, so I had to be a man and let her go if that's what she wanted.

"Can you please just call me when you make it to where you going?"

She shook her head no then walked out. I watched as she packed her suitcases into the car before she got in and drove off. I closed the door then punched a hole into the living room wall. I fucked up and it wasn't shit I could do to fix it. I went upstairs to grab my keys and headed out the door.

Chapter Nineteen

Khadijah

I didn't have to ring the bell as I walked up to Angel's door because I told her to stay up for me. She came out up and grabbed two of my suitcases and we tip toed to the guest room so we wouldn't wake the kids. Sitting the suitcases on the floor, I sat on the bed then Angel sat next to me rubbing my back.

"You okay?"

"No."

"It's okay sis, everything will be okay. Get you some rest, you don't have to worry about Jr. I will keep him until you're feeling a bit better."

"Okay, thanks Ang."

She got up and walked out, closing the door behind her. I just laid on the queen size mattress and cried. I gave him all of me and I just don't understand why would he do this to me. With all of the kids he has on the way I've never left his side. Maybe giving your all to a person and trusting them is a rule that should not be used.

My phone began ringing and it was Yatta, so I hit the silent button as I just stared at the wall 'til I fell asleep.

The morning came and the sunlight was shining bright, too bad I didn't feel that way inside. I got up and went to the bathroom right across from the room. Doing my morning hygiene routine, I finished my shower and I walked back to the room with my towel wrapped around then locked the door as I got dressed.

Shatavia

After putting on my bra and underwear, I slipped on some blue jeans and a blue crop top. I left my curly hair down after spraying some oil sheen on it. I slipped on some all-white Forces then walked out while checking my phone.

"Mommy!!"

I put my phone in my back pocket as my baby boy ran up to me and I picked him up giving him all of my kisses.

"Where you going mommy?"

"Mommy has to go handle business today, but I will be back and we can watch movies and make pizza!"

"Yayyy!"

I put Jr. down as I walked into the kitchen where my sister was making breakfast.

Jr. tapped my leg and asked, "Where's daddy?"

Right before I could answer my phone started to ring and it was Yatta. I walked to the porch and answered the call.

"What?"

"Baby why haven't you been picking up I been calling you to check on you and Jr."

"I'm not your baby and we are good."

I hate that I had to be angry with him, but I wanted him to learn not to play with my feelings so I had to play hard.

"I have a surprise for you."

"I don't want any surprises and I don't need anything from you."

"Dijah I understand you're upset, but can you just give me a chance baby, please."

"No."

Just when I said no I seen his BMW pull into the parking lot with a pink one pulling up right behind him and I shook my head. I hung my phone up and proceeded to walk back into the house, but he got out and grabbed me right before I twisted the door knob.

"Baby I'm sorry I hurt you, okay? I wasn't thinking, but I'm willing to do whatever it is you need me to do so we can get back on good terms."

"I need time to myself because you cheated and I'm not about to take you back with open arms."

"I know baby, but I can't live without you. Dijah I know I messed up baby, but I'm willing to work on this. I really do love you."

I turned my head away from him and tears began to fall down my face. I wiped them then look back up at him.

"I hope you don't think buying me a BMW was gone butter me up to go back with you."

"It's a gift sweetheart."

A smile crept on my face as he handed me the keys.

"I'm willing to wait on you."

"Thank you."

We hugged and his grip around me felt so good, but I didn't want to show him any signs of weakness so I stepped back.

"How did you even know where I was?"

"Research."

I looked at Yatta and he looked rough like he hadn't had any sleep, but he still looked good with his dreads hanging.

"So could we at least still talk or you don't want to communicate with me at all?"

"We can still communicate Yatta."

"Okay, I will talk to you later."

"Okay, thank you again for the car."

"You don't have to thank me."

He walked off and I wanted to just pack my things up and leave with him but I had to put my foot down. When he drove off I looked at the keys that were in my hand with a keychain hanging from it with my name on it in silver letters. I went to check out the car and it was so beautiful, the rims had pink in them mixed with black. I used the key to unlock the door and I sat in the front seat admiring the pink and black leather interior and I was lost for words. I wiped tears away from my face and walked back inside.

"What was that all about?" my sister asked and I held up my keys.

"He bought you a new car!"

"It's outside."

I watched as she rushed to the window to see and she began jumping up and down.

"Girl that is so fucking beautiful. You better take your ass back home to that man and lay it on him."

"I have to let him know gifts are not a way to apologize. He has to know not to do this shit to me again and sex don't mean shit, I give him that regularly and he still fucked around on me."

"You got a point because some men do think if 'I buy her such and such' everything gone be cool then they end up doing the same shit again."

"Right, and I'm not for that."

"You talked to ma?"

"Nope, you?"

"Yeah, I spoke to her last night."

"You got daddy number?" I asked her.

"No, I didn't ask for it but I talked to ma and she said he was just over there."

"Right, they trying to get back together and shit."

We both began laughing then the kids came into the room.

"Y'all want to go to grandma's house today?" I asked them and they all said yeah.

I looked at Angel and she must have been thinking just like me because she already had them dressed, so I packed Jr.'s bag and she packed her kids' bags too. When we were finished, I took everything out to my old car and strapped the kids in their seatbelts as Angel got in on the passenger side.

When I arrived at my mom's house, I got the kids out of the back seat along with their bags with the help of Angel. I walked up to the porch holding Jr.'s hand and Angel was right behind me with her two.

Shatavia

My mom opened the door smiling from ear to ear and I knew her and my daddy were back fucking around.

"Hey my babies!"

"They wanted to spend some time with their grandma today."

"Well that's no problem, I hardly see them anyway. Where you two going?"

"We're going to take care of some business, we will pick them up tonight."

"Okay, come on granny's babies."

The kids ran inside and we handed her their bags.

"I will call you when we are on our way back to pick them up ma," Angel said.

"Okay, you two be careful."

We raced back to the car and I headed back to Angel's so we could get in my new BMW and go shopping for some new clothes. Then we were going to the shop to get our hair and nails done.

Tonya

"Ma hold on a second, I'll be right back."

I was supposed to be giving my mother her medicine, but the urge to throw up came over me and I ran to the nearest bathroom and threw up everything I had just ate.

After I was done, I rinsed my mouth out and wiped my face with a wash cloth that I put under warm water. Walking back into my mother's room, she was now sitting up looking at me as I walked over to her dresser to get her medicine. My mother had a breast cancer scare a few months ago. The doctor had to perform surgery and took the lump out for testing, but it came back negative. She now has a house nurse that comes to monitor what she eats and how she takes care of herself. I gave her the medicine with a bottle of cold water. She took them and looked up at me.

"So are you still with the child's father?" she asked.

I felt uncomfortable talking to my mother about my situation and I just wasn't ready to speak on it yet.

"I'm not pregnant ma, just the stomach flu."

"Child please, who do you think you're talking to?"

I held my head down and sat next to her. I loved my mother but I'm not sure if we could ever get back that close bond we use to have. The day she told me I'm responsible for her being lonely hurt me so bad. At the end of the day I know she loves me and I love her, you only get one mother.

"Ma everything just not going right for me anymore."

"He left you?"

"Yeah, well no, he was killed and I'm eighteen weeks. I just found out I was pregnant yesterday, I can't do this ma."

"You just have to thank God nothing happened to that gift He's blessed you with. Be thankful he gave you another day to see. I know you wish the child's father was here with you and it's unfortunate he had to die that way, but you know God makes no mistakes. So from now on you have to think about that baby you're carrying, he or she is going to be looking up to you. I know I wasn't the best mother, but I made sure you never needed or wanted for nothing My thing was I didn't know how to show you love as you got older and I'm truly sorry for that. Just take that as a lesson and become the best mother you could be to your unborn."

Tears rolled down my face as I stared at her and every word she said to me hit me emotionally. I couldn't help but hug her as she held me tight in her embrace. I cried like a little girl and I was happy that my mother finally apologized for how she treated me over the years; I just felt loved but emotional and hurt at my situation.

Unique

"This bitch is not answering her phone," I said to Tasha as I called Mary's phone back to back but kept getting the voicemail.

"Maybe Yatta caught on."

"Not unless she ran her fuckin' mouth but I doubt that shit."

After I called three more time and ended up with the same results, I gave up. I got up and grabbed a few pieces of Popeye's chicken that Tasha bought and sat on the couch with her.

"Why won't you just give up on this shit and focus on how you gone provide for them babies when they get here."

"Because he thinks he can get away with anything. Plus we still throwing the baby shower and they gone be straight for a while."

I ate my chicken then watched Tasha as she shook her head. I hear where she was coming from, but Yatta walked around like he's king or some shit. After he chocked and hit me the other day, he deserved to be killed; him and that yellow ass bitch Khadijah. Feeling like my plan back fired on me, I grabbed the phone and dialed Nick's number.

"What's up?"

"I need to come speak to you."

"A'ight I'm on the block right now, give a me an hour. I gotta make my end today."

"Okay."

Nick was a young nigga that's been working for Yatta. He's actually the one that told me where the trap was when I bumped into him some days ago. I felt like I had to get this over with, but another part of me wanted to just give up and be with him again so I'd have our family. I knew that wasn't going to happen, so my only plan was to have him and that bitch killed.

"Bitch you don't need to be going nowhere as big as you are."

"I'm six months, it's good to stay fit."

"Whatever."

Tasha shook her head as she walked to her room, and I finished my chicken then jumped in the shower.

Ken

I got dressed and headed out to my car. When I arrived to Rich's crib, I made sure to roll my windows up and lock my car doors.

"What's going on Rich?"

"Shit, been chilling."

I walked inside and we sat in the front room where he had a laptop placed in front of him and turned it around to me.

"You seen this young nigga before?"

I looked at the picture.

"That's my daughters' boyfriend."

"I pulled up some information on him and it looks like he could be a suspect in your brother's murder."

"What information is that?"

"Well I know for a fact that he and his brother used to sell drugs for Greg when he was a shorty. They were all close but as they got older, dude's brother began taking over the streets so it was some shit about his brother getting killed. Greg was behind that shit so dude probably retaliated and killed Greg."

I sat back on the couch processing everything he just told me. It all made since because I knew how my brother could be when it came down to money and I knew how his ego was. I don't care what my brother did, but they crossed the line fucking with my family.

"What else you got on this nigga?"

"He owns a barbershop in the 100s by that beauty salon."

"A'ight. I'll catch up with you later Rich, thanks."

"It's no problem, but you don't need me to roll with you?"

"No, you know I'm good."

"A'ight, I'll see you around bro."

"Good looking."

I walked out and headed over to the barbershop. I made sure my Glock was fully loaded. I knew Khadijah loved him, but she probably didn't know what he's done to her uncle and I was going to take things into my own hands.

Chapter Twenty

Kenyatta

Finishing up on my costumer's head, I gave him a mirror so he could check out the new cut before he paid me my money. When he was walking out Jay was walking in.

"What's up bro?"

"Shit, just trying to cut a few heads before the day over with."

"True. What you on when you get off?"

"Shit chilling, Dijah still mad at me so I'm just gone chill and get high."

"That's yo fault bro I told yo ass not to tell her."

"I know but I really love her and lying to her is just something I can't do."

"Well you should come to the club with me tonight."

"Hell naw, I'm good."

"Damn you don't want to kick it tonight just so you could get some ass or something bro."

"No, I'm good."

"Damn, you in love with shorty that much?"

"Hell yeah, she the one for me."

I watched as Jay shook his head and in walked Khadijah's father with a frown on his face.

"I need to speak with you in private," he came over and said to me.

"Aye I'll be back Jay."

"A'ight."

I walked him to the back where my office was and closed the door.

"You want to take a seat?" I asked as I sat down behind my desk.

"No, I came to talk to you about some things."

"Okay, and what's that?"

"I don't appreciate you treating my baby girl this way."

I scrunched my face up at the fact that Dijah told him I cheated on her, but she told me they weren't even that close.

"You kill her uncle then try to date her? What type of shit is that?"

"What are you talking about?"

I stood up just in case his old ass felt like upping on my ass.

"You killed my brother, Greg, now it's your time. Hope you get to see your brother."

He reached behind him and grabbed his gun and I ducked as he aimed it towards me. He let off two shots but missed. When I got back up he aimed and shot me in my arm. I grabbed my gun and aimed it at him and popped him in the leg right as Jay bust in. Before he could let off another round Jay shot him in the head.

"Noooo!" I yelled and punched the wall.

"What the fuck you mean no, he was just trying to kill you!"

"That's Khadijah's father bro! Fuck!"

"A'ight, you told me the nigga wasn't even in her life like that."

"Still bro… Fuck man!"

"Ima call the crew."

I walked out of the office while blood dropped from my injured arm.

"Everything okay boss?"

"Yeah, but I'm gone have to close down early so y'all pack your things"

They all had a look on their face as if they'd seen a ghost and began to pack up their belongings.

"So when do we return?"

"Y'all can come back on Monday, I will have a meeting about the shop."

They all nodded their heads and walked out talking amongst themselves. I went back to the back and looked at Jay as he ended the call with the clean crew.

"I gotta move the shop."

"Why is that?"

"I don't need another scene like this happening at my place of business."

"I hear you."

I gave Jay the keys to lockup as I walked out and got inside of my car, then headed to the nearest hospital. After they took care of my arm, I exited the building and walked to my car, but I stopped once I saw Unique's ass walking inside of the hospital.

"Unique!"

She turned around and the look on her face told me she was up to something as she walked over to me.

"What's up Yatta? What happened to your arm?"

"Don't worry about but I know yo' ass tried to have worse done to me."

She looked at me with guilt in her eyes and I got hot, but didn't want to cause a scene in the hospital parking lot.

"Just wait 'til you have them babies, yo' ass is dead, bitch."

I turned around, got in my car, and drove to my house. When I got there I went straight for my loud and blunts and began rolling up. I then grabbed my Hennessy from the cabinet and went back up to my room. Drowning out my thoughts and the events that just occurred, I began smoking and drinking.

Khadijah

After getting our hair and nails done, we headed back to our mother's house. I loved my new look, I dyed my hair an auburn color and I couldn't stop admiring it. I got Jr. gifts while we were out shopping and also I got me a whole new wardrobe.

"You want me to get the kids?"

"Yeah," I told my sister.

I loved my sister's new look as well. She had her hair curled and got honey blond streaks. Before she got out the door my mom was calling.

"Yeah ma, we outside."

"I was calling to tell you that they could stay the night."

"You sure?"

"Yeah they are no trouble. I rarely get to see them and they are having a good time with me, just come get them in the morning."

"Okay."

I hung the phone up and grabbed Angel as she was about to get out.

"She said they spending the night."

"Okay, so what you about to do?"

I wanted so bad to tell her I was going home but I didn't want her judging me.

"I'm about to go handle business, you want me to drop you off at home?"

"Yeah."

I started the car back up then headed back to her house. When I got to her driveway she got out and got her bags along with her kids' new clothes and toys. I helped her put the things up in her house with promises that I would call her later. Getting back in my car I drove down to my girl Tonya's mama house to check on her.

There was a gang of niggas on the block when I stepped out of my car and what I had on didn't save my thick ass from them trying to spit game. Ignoring them, I rang the doorbell and waited for Tee to open the door. While waiting one of the guys walked over to me. He was sexy in his own way but he wasn't Yatta.

"Hey sweetheart, you looking lovely today."

"Thank you."

"My name is Von by the way beautiful, what's yours?"

Before I could respond, Tonya opened her door and I went right in. I waited on her to close and lock the door then hugged Tonya and sat down on the couch.

"How's mom?" I asked as she sat on the small couch across from me.

"She's good, she's sleep right now."

"But look at you though, looking like a different person. I almost didn't recognize you."

We both laughed.

"Yeah I had to try something different."

"I feel you."

"How you been?"

"Okay, my doctor's appointment is in about two weeks. That's the appointment I get to see what I'm having."

"Yasss, I'm coming too. Just let me know what time, I will be here to pick you up and all. You know I'm gone spoil the shit out my God baby."

We laughed again but I was dead serious.

"You been okay though?"

"Not really but I'm going to get better."

"I wish I could make you feel better, best friend."

"It's all good. Eventually, I will get over it and be okay."

"How you and Yatta doing, and how's Jr.?"

"Jr.'s fine but Yatta and I aren't on the best of terms right now."

"What did he do?"

"Cheated with some bitch the other day. Then he thinks that buying me that nice ass BMW was gone win me over."

Tonya got up and looked out her window to see my pink BMW and looked back over at me with wide eyes.

"Girl, that damn BMW nice ass fuck! Shit if I were you, I would be throwing ass back with no problem."

Laughing at her funny ass, she sat back down.

"That'll be soon but it's I don't want him to think that shit is okay to do then think buying shit like that is supposed to make it better."

"I feel you on that."

"You're not interested in Jay?"

I watched as a smirk came across her face then she started to blush giving me my answer.

"I mean, he's nice looking and all but I don't think I could be able to date him Dijah."

"Why, because he was Chris's friend?"

"Yeah."

"Well you never know, he could be the one for you."

"Girl I'm about to have a baby. That man ain't gone want to deal with that shit, he doesn't seem like the type."

"Like I said, you never know. So you have a baby on the way, my son about to be two years old next month and you see him and Yatta bond like they blood. IF he really likes you he'd treat yours just like it was his."

"I don't know if he's that type though. Some niggas don't want to deal with a female and a child that's not his."

"Girl I understand that but not all guys are like that."

"I guess."

"I was just dropping by to check in on you. Do you need anything?"

"No, I'm good."

"You sure?"

"Yes."

I got up and walked to the door.

"Give me a hug," I said to her reaching my arms out.

When she hugged me I was hoping that it would make her feel a little better.

"I'm going to see you Monday at work, right?"

"Yeah of course, I'm not missing out on my money."

"I know that's right. Well I will see you then."

"Okay, drive safe, don't mess that sexy thang up."

We both bust out laughing as I walked to my car. I got in and started the car as I watched Tee walk back inside of the house before I pulled off, heading home to my baby. I'm not going to lie, I missed his ass; I just had to talk to him and let his ass know if there was one more fuck up, I was gone for good. When I arrived I spotted his car in the driveway so I got out and used my house key.

Closing and locking the door I made my way upstairs to the bedroom. Since the hallways were so dark in here, I cut on a light then turned it off when I made it to the top of the staircase. Walking in the room, I turned on the light and Yatta was sitting up with nothing but his boxers on, drinking Hennessy from the bottle and smoking a blunt.

"Why are you just sitting in the dark? How can you see?"

I sat next to him and he looked at me as if I was a brand new person, forgetting that I dyed my hair.

"Damn baby, you look beautiful. You look like a whole different female."

I smiled and moved closer to him and noticed his arm was wrapped up.

"What happened to your arm Yatta?"

"Playing around and messed myself up at the shop, I'm a'ight. When did you do that to your hair? I like it."

"I got it done earlier and thank you."

"I want to say to you that I'm really sorry for everything and the pain I've caused you."

"It's okay baby, but I want you to know that if you have one more careless fuck up happen, I will be done for good," I said firmly so he knew I wasn't playing.

"You got my word. Matter of fact, I'm not even going to say anything else because I will show you from here on out."

"Where's my little man?"

"He's at my moms, I went shopping and got him a few early birthday gifts."

"Yeah, his birthday is coming up. I gotta get him some shit."

We both looked at each other as the room got quite.

"I'm trying to get like you," I said as I pointed to the bottle of half drunken Hennessy.

He passed me the bottle and I took a big gulp as he rolled another blunt, then sparked it up and passed it to me after a few pulls.

"I really missed yo' ass Dijah."

I blew the smoke out of my mouth then looked at him.

"I've missed you too baby, but you know you really hurt me."

He stood up from the bed moving his dreads out of his face, towering over me as I smoked the blunt. He softly pushed me back onto the bed and pulled my pants down. His kisses started at my stomach then trailed down to my thighs as he kissed each inner thigh slowly and then kissed my womanhood. I moaned out in pleasure as I smoked the blunt.

Catching me off guard, he went in and began eating me out, making me moan louder as I grabbed his dreads with my free hand and pushed his face further in. After my third nut, Yatta got up and had my wetness all around his mouth. He wiped it off with his towel he had nearby and took off his boxers. I put out the blunt and laid back down on the bed, away from my mess that I made. He climbed on top of me with his manhood standing at attention.

He began kissing me passionately and I felt an unexplainable feeling come over me as he pushed himself inside of me slowly while whispering in my ear that he loved me; he had me in tears. This making love shit had me feeling too good. I loved this man with everything in me and I probably gave in too easy, but I couldn't help it. I believe that this time around he would get his shit together.

After we got through making love, I took my shirt off and laid on the bed. Yatta laid next to me and we passed the bottle back and forth.

"I been meaning to tell you some shit."

"Like what?" I asked, looking over at him.

"You remember I told you about that bitch from out of town that was supposed to be pregnant with my baby?"

"Yeah."

"She called me one day and told me she wasn't even pregnant."

"And how you know that for sure?"

"Because the bitch had the nerve to ask if I could come back down there to make one with her."

"Oh wow."

"I know, you the one I want carrying my baby."

"Yeah, but I still don't want that to happen because Unique still has your twins on the way."

"I don't know if they're mine yet."

"I guess."

I laid back and looked up at the ceiling, drifting off in my own thoughts 'til Yatta started back talking.

"I really appreciate you being by my side, baby."

"I know you do."

"You're my soulmate and I'm never giving up on you, no matter what."

"You mean that?"

"Hell yeah, you my everything."

"Why don't you tell me that while I ride you?" I said with a smile on my face.

Feeling the liquor, I got up and straddled him then slid his hard dick inside of me as I bounced up and down on him.

"You my everything Dijah."

He smacked both of my ass cheeks and we made love 'til the sunrise.

Chapter Twenty-One

Khadijah

It's been a month and Jr.'s party was this weekend. I been working my ass off at the salon even though I had plenty of money saved up. There was nothing wrong with making extra. Today I got off early, so I headed over to my sister's to pick up my baby.

When I arrived, he came running to my car. I got out and he jumped into my arms and I hugged him before I put him in his seat.

Me and my sister exchanged a few words before I got in and headed home. Like always Jr., was asleep before we got to the house. I pulled up and got him out of the car and carried him up the steps, into the house. After laying him on his bed, I closed his door and went back downstairs to take out some chicken that was in the refrigerator. As I seasoned the meat, ty phone began ringing.

"Hello?"

"Hey baby."

"Hey, when are you coming home?"

"I will be there in a few, just checking on you."

"Okay, well I'm about to start on dinner."

"Alright baby, I'll be there soon."

"Okay."

I hung up and went back to preparing the dinner for tonight which was baked chicken, cornbread, spaghetti and broccoli. An hour later I finished dinner just as Jr. woke up from his late nap.

"Mommy, where is daddy?"

"He will be here in a second baby. You ready to eat eat?"

"Yeah!"

I fixed Jr.'s plate then sat him down at the table to eat then fixed my own and put Yatta's plate in the microwave. Before I could sit down, Yatta came in looking sexy as fuck. Getting up, I ran over to him with Jr. in the background yelling daddy as I kissed all over him. Closing and locking the door, I walked back to the kitchen to get his plate as he picked Jr. up talking to him. I warmed his plate up and sat back at the dinner table and we ate while Jr. watched his favorite show, Bubble Guppies.

After we were done with dinner I took the plates into the kitchen and placed them on the right side of the sink as I began to get the water ready to wash dishes. Yatta walked up behind me, grabbed me by the waist and kissed my neck.

"Baby I'm going to get little man ready for bed, make sure you take off all your clothes before you lay down."

I laughed as he whispered the last part in my ear making me hot.

"Shut up Ya," I said as I moved him a little bit off me.

He laughed and hit my ass as he walked away, picking up Jr. and taking him upstairs to the bathroom so he could bathe him.

Yatta and I were doing good and I couldn't ask for anything better. For Jr.'s party was this weekend, we planned on having a jump house in the back and a few of the Bubble Guppies characters to stop by. The only thing I had left to do was invite more children.

Jay

After getting up doing my morning routine, I woke Tissa up so she could roll with me to the store to get some more house items. I had already dressed for the day so I waited for Tissa. Me and Tissa been messing around for a good year now, and I admit I did some foul shit with cheating on her and putting my hands on her in the past, but I promised her I would make it up to her and that's what I been doing.

"Baby can we stop by the nail shop, I wanted to get my nails done."

"No problem."

Tissa was bad as fuck; her brown complexion brought out her hazel eyes and she had hips and ass for day with a beautiful, natural ass face. Tissa was into that weave shit and that's the only part I hated about her. She would rock her natural hair a few times out the month, but most of the time you would catch her wearing that weave. Don't get me wrong, she still looked sexy in it but that shit be breaking my fuckin' pockets with the expensive ass hair she gets instead of her just wearing her own.

Tissa works for a clinic down the street from Yatta's shop and I support my baby at whatever she did because most females just like to sit around and think money supposed to just fall from the sky and into their lap, or use a Nigga as a ATM. I buy her shit, even though she has her own money, because that's my baby; I still do it just because.

Getting in my BMW, we headed over to Walmart and found a parking space. As we out walked into the store Tissa stayed close to me. While walking to the laundry detergent aisle I spotted Tonya, and I wasn't going to lie, she was looking gorgeous as hell in her blue sundress and her hair pinned up, showing off her beautiful face. I held my head down so she wouldn't notice me.

"Baby I will be back, I'm going to get my female products and I'll meet you back over here in a few."

"Okay."

When she was out of site, I looked up and spotted Tonya looking at me, but turned away once we caught each other's glances. I walked over to her and she tried avoiding me, but that didn't work.

"How you doing Tonya?"

"I'm fine Jay."

I could tell she had a little attitude and that's probably because she seen me with Tissa.

"What you getting today?" I asked her as I looked in her shopping cart and spotted infant clothes.

"Just things I need."

"Ah okay, well it was nice seeing you, beautiful."

"Same."

She said as she proceeded to walk off but I stopped her.

"Aye, why don't you give me your number so we could talk some time?"

"Your girlfriend gone get mad about that, I'm good."

"She don't care Tonya."

We stared at each other for a minute before I handed her my phone so she could put her number in. After she was finished she walked away and I walked down the aisle to look for the detergent.

After a day of shopping for the house and getting Tissa's nails done, a nigga was tired. I left Tissa at home to put all that shit up and went out to the car to roll my weed up. I began driving once I was finished and flamed up. Driving with no destination, I decided to pull over by a gas station and pulled out my phone. Just as I was about to dial Tonya's number, I spotted Nick and Unique chitchatting in a car together, but they were so deep off into their conversation they didn't even notice me before they pulled off. I shook my head at how trifling this bitch, Unique was. I never thought she was that type of female and it's sad because she's trying to mess up Yatta's life.

I made a note to myself to holla at Yatta about that shit while I continued to smoke my blunt and called Tonya. She answered it on the fourth ring.

"Hello?"

"Damn you sound even sexier on the phone," I honestly said as she smacked her lips.

"What's up though. what you doing?"

"Nothing, just got through putting a few things up."

"That's cool. You got some free time?"

"Yeah, but we could meet up somewhere else."

"You want me to come get you or you want to drive and meet me?"

"I could drive, just give me the location."

"No, I rather come and get you. What's your address?"

After she gave me her address, which wasn't that far from where I was, I was on my way to her. Pulling up, I saw her beautiful ass sitting on the porch, and she came down and got in the car soon as she saw me.

"What's up, lovely?"

"Nothing much. So where we headed to?" she asked me, and I was just stuck looking at her sexy beautiful chocolate ass.

"Um hellooo?"

"I'm sorry, you asked where we going?"

"Yes."

"To my spot."

"Okay."

She buckled herself in her seatbelt and I began to drive to my second crib. I usually use my second crib if me and Tissa get into it or something. Other than that I really don't spend too much time in it, but I still make sure the bills and shit are paid. Arriving, we got out and walked inside my place.

"I like this, it's really nice."

"Thank you."

"Do you drink or smoke?"

"No."

I was shocked because most females around her age do both. We sat down on my grey sectional and just looked at each other for a while. It was something about Tonya that lit a spark inside me whenever I saw her, and that's been ever since she was fucking around with Chris's bitch ass. I guess he caught on because he had stopped her from coming around whenever we had meetings and shit at his crib.

"So what do you like to do?"

"I like to do hair, read, and cook. What do you like to do?"

"Well I'm a street pharmacist, that's how I make my money so you could say I like to make money."

"Don't we all."

I nodded my head and looked into her eyes.

"So why did you want to see me, you sure your girlfriend not gone get mad?"

Although I knew damn well Tissa was gone get mad if she found out I was talking to Tonya, I decided to play a role like we really weren't feeling each other.

"Naw, she has her male friends and I don't trip and it's the same with me."

"Oh."

I sat closer to her and it seemed as if she tensed up.

"How you been lately though?"

"I been okay. So why do you have me here if you have a girlfriend? I'm not that type to fuck on you when you're in a relationship, so if you looking to get some ass from me then I'm already letting you know it's a dead mission."

I had to pause and laugh at her for a second because I just asked her one thing and she just went in on me.

"Listen, I know you been feeling me since day one so don't even try to act like you wouldn't give it up to me if I asked. Next, I'm not even trying to get on that fucking shit with you because I just want to get to know you better first."

"Well I'm just letting you know I'm not with that side chick shit."

"I would never put you in that position."

I watched as she moved over a bit from me and that's when I noticed her belly.

"You pregnant?"

She had a look on her face that told me she was before she even said anything.

"Yeah, I am."

"How far along are you?"

"Five and a half."

"You know what you having?"

"Not yet, in a week or so I go back to find out."

At that moment a feeling inside of me washed over me and I didn't like it at all. The fact that Tonya was pregnant, bringing a baby into this world with no father had me feeling bad. I knew how it felt to grow up without a father and instead of going down the right path, I chose to do this street shit because I had no guidance from a man. My mother raised me the best she could, but she just couldn't get me on the right track.

"How are you taking the pregnancy with everything that's happened?"

I looked at her sincerely and she began to cry. I moved over to her and just held her as I rocked her back and forth. I felt her pain because I know my mother went through the same shit; I hated to see her cry just like how I hate to see Tonya break down.

"Look, everything will be good, okay? You need anything, I will be there. You need anyone to go to doctor's appointments with you, I will be there too. You don't have to go through this alone."

Her crying began to come to a stop and she looked up at me.

"I wouldn't want you or expect you to do anything like that though."

"I know you wouldn't, I just know off experience this shit is not right. I grew up without a father and I don't want he or she to know what that feeling is at all."

She hugged me tight and the connection our bodies shared made me realize she could probably be the one for me. After a little more conversation, we wrapped it up around seven-thirty at night and I drove her home. When I got back home I went upstairs to see where Tissa was, but come to my surprise she was in the middle of packing her bags and shit.

"Aye, what the fuck you doing?"

"I'm not going through this shit with you again Jay."

"What the fuck are you talking about?"

"You out fucking around on me again, I can feel it, I know you gave that chick your number up at the store earlier, I just didn't say shit because I wanted to see what you were going to do when I got back."

I sat on the bed and watched her pack up her things and a part of me wanted to stop her, but the other part was just saying fuck it. I know I put her threw a lot over the year we were together and she deserved someone better than me.

"I know what I've done to you over the past year wasn't right, but I have nothing but love for you and I'm not mad at you for your decision to leave me."

I watched Tissa continue to pack as tears fell from her eyes. I got up and hugged her, but she pushed me away.

"I don't want to speak to you ever again!"

With those words being said, she walked out with her bags and I sat back on the bed with my hands over my face. I heard the door slam then seconds later her car pulled out of my driveway.

Chapter Twenty-Two

Khadijah

Today was Jr.'s party and I invited all family and friends to come out with their kids so they could help celebrate my baby's birthday.

"Who's birthday is it today?" I asked Jr. all excited as he walked into my bedroom rubbing his eyes.

I could tell he was still sleepy, so I picked him up and laid him in between Yatta and I. Seconds later their asses were snoring together, causing me to get up out the bed. Since I wasn't sleepy anymore I decided to make breakfast.

Before I could get down the steps, I ran to the bathroom throwing up my insides into the toilet. After I was done, I began to rinse my mouth out and proceeded to the kitchen to make breakfast. After finishing up the pancakes, eggs, bacon, biscuits, and grits, I started to walk up the stairs to wake the guys, but they were already woke coming down with Yatta holding a now wide awake Jr.

"Good morning baby, you got it smelling good in here."

"Of course, happy birthday big boy!" I said to Jr. as Yatta handed him to me.

"How old are you big man?" Yatta asked Jr.

"Two!" he said, and we both began clapping and cheering him on for knowing his age.

My baby boy was growing up on me. I sat Jr. down at the table and cut on his favorite show as I began making his plate. Yatta's loud ass phone began to ring causing me to look at him, but I continued making Jr.'s plate as I tried to ear hustle.

"You saw what? ... How the fuck is that even possible? ... A'ight bro, I will talk to you later about it, my son party today. You still coming through? ... A'ight bet."

After he hung up the phone, I sat Jr.'s plate in front of him and he began to eat as I walked over to Yatta who was making his plate.

"You okay?"

"Yeah."

I could tell he wasn't okay just by his body language but I let it go because today was Jr.'s day and I don't want anything ruining it.

After we were finished with our breakfast, I bathed Jr. as Yatta washed the dishes and cleaned up the kitchen. I dressed Jr. in his Nike outfit and put on his new, white Nike shoes. Once he was dressed, I sat him in his room to play with his toys while I got in the shower and got dressed.

It was now midday and everyone arrived with their children. My baby was having a blast with his cousins and friends in the jump house, so I walked over to the back porch and sat in the chair as I watched them have a good time. Before I could take a sip of my water, Tonya tapped me on my back surprising me.

"I thought you weren't going to come," I said as I got up to hug her, looking at what she had on.

"You know I wouldn't miss my nephew's birthday party for nothing. Where do I put this?" she asked holding his big present in her hand.

"I will take that. Why you trying to hide my baby?"

She looked down at her black dress and looked back up at me smiling.

"Because I don't want no one to know yet."

"Girl bye, they gone know eventually."

She sat next to me and her glow had me smile right along with her.

"So where's Jr.?"

"He's in that jump house playing with his cousins and friends having a ball. So when you going to find out the sex of the baby?"

"I go Monday, so hopefully the baby act right so the doctor can find out."

"Well I bought unisex clothes so I'm just waiting to find out what we having to splurge."

We both laughed and Yatta came walking out with Jay. I watched Tee and Jay as they stared at each other looking like secret love birds.

"Baby, I'm about to go get the cake and ice cream. I will be right back."

"Okay baby."

"I told yo' ass I could have went, but since you insist then okay," my sister said to Yatta as she walked from the house to the back porch with us.

"You know I got this sis, just relax."

Yatta gave me a kiss then him and Jay walked off into the front of the house.

"Heyyy Tonya, girl how you been!" Angel asked her as she sat down in a chair between us.

"I been good. How you been?"

"Girl I been straight, taking care of my bad ass kids. I never thought y'all would get back in contact."

"Yeah, we work at the same salon. Dijah first day there she acted like she ain't even remember me," Tonya said with a smile on her face.

"I didn't, you looked different than what I was use too," I said as we all laughed.

We watched the kids enjoy themselves and talked about the old days, waiting on Yatta to get back with the cake and ice cream.

Yatta

"So what the fuck you mean you saw them at the gas station together?"

"They ass was conversing and didn't notice me, I know what I saw."

"We gotta handle this shit asap, his ass probably the one telling her all the shit."

I shook my head as we arrived at the cake shop. Stepping in, I gave the baker my information and paid for the expensive ass spider man cake. The cake was decent as hell, I don't see how they baked the shit.

"I don't want to mess the cake up in my car, y'all deliver?"

"Yes sir, we deliver. What's the address?"

I gave him the address and he typed some keys on his computer's keyboard.

"Okay sir, that would be an extra twenty dollars."

"Okay no problem, but I need this cake delivered asap," I said as I paid him the money, waiting on him to return the receipt.

"Okay sir."

Jay and I walked out and got back in the car, heading over to store to get ice cream. Once we got the ice cream we headed back to my spot and I stopped at the gas station to get some backwoods.

"What's up bitch nigga, you thought it was over?"

I instantly went for my gun and turned around, but before I could shoot he shot me in my leg and I collapsed. He tried running, but I shot his ass in his shoulder. He held it as he ran out of the station. I saw Jay getting out bussing at his ass but he got away.

Looking at the terrified people hiding in the back, I tried to get up but failed. Jay walked in helping me up and into the car.

"Man what the fuck!" he asked as he helped me in the passenger's seat, driving to the nearest hospital.

"That nigga has to die, I'm done playing games with that bitch. I was trying to spare his life because of the simple fact that he's Jr.'s father, but fuck that shit man! Fuck!" I yelled holding my wounded leg as blood poured out.

"Damn man, I couldn't even hit is ass but we definitely gonna get that nigga," Jay said as we arrived at the hospital.

Filling out all my information, I paid the doctors and nurses extra to speed up the process. After getting the bullet removed from my lower calf and getting the wound cleaned up, the doctors told me to come back within two weeks to check on the healing process. I quickly learned how to use the crutches the doctor gave me after one tutorial.

Signing the discharge papers and getting my prescription, I walked out to the car with the crutches and Dijah was blowing my phone up. I got in the passenger side and let Jay drive me to the Walgreens pharmacy and picked up my pills and headed back home.

Arriving home, I checked around back and everyone was gone so I walked inside the house.

"Dijah!" I called, as Jay walked in behind me, closing the door and sitting down next to me as I put my crutches up.

"Baby! Oh my god! What happened to your leg!"

"I got shot, but I'll be good. Where Jr. at?"

"My mom kept him and his cousins for the rest of the weekend since he was so eager to leave me. But who did this to you?" she asked sitting next to me looking concerned.

I looked over at Jay and he looked at me, then back at Dijah and she peeped what we were doing.

"So nobody's going to say anything?" she asked looking at the both of us.

"I can't tell you that."

"Why the fuck not!"

"Because I don't want you in my business, Dijah."

She got up, walked to the bedroom, and slammed the door. She just didn't understand this street shit wasn't for her and I didn't want her getting involved in any way because her baby daddy was the one that shot me.

"Man bro, you good?"

"Yeah man, I will be straight but that mission still on about buddy ass."

"A'ight bet, I'll talk to you later."

We shook hands and he walked out. I grabbed my crutches and walked over to lock the door then cut off the lights downstairs. I cut on the hallway light and carefully made my way upstairs to the bedroom.

When I finally made it up the stairs, I cut the hallway light off and opened the door to the bedroom to find Khadijah's ass rolling up my shit.

"Who told yo ass to go through my stash?"

She rolled her eyes at me and rolled a third blunt up before she put my shit back up and began flaming up. I sighed and sat down on the bed next to her, lifting my injured leg up on the bed as I watched her smoke.

"Baby?" I said to her.

"What?" she asked with attitude in her voice.

"You mad at me now?"

"Of course Yatta, you just got shot but don't want to tell me by who? You know I have to walk out on them same streets you walking and I have to look out for myself and Jr. as well. Motherfuckers know we a couple and could make us a target so I have the right to know."

I go where she was coming from, but I still wasn't going to tell her who because I can handle the shit.

"I understand that baby, one hundred percent but just know I got this. I don't want you to be involved in anything I do. Just know you and Jr. gone always be straight."

"I know that, but what if it would have been worse?"

"Don't think like that, I'm gone always be around."

"Whatever Yatta. I hate this street shit you in."

"Baby, look at me," I said to her as I grabbed her chin, turning her face towards me.

"We gone be good, okay?"

She was hesitant but she nodded her head.

"Okay."

We kissed and she passed me the blunt. I took a few hits and we laid back, enjoying each other's company as we talked about our future.

Chapter Twenty-Three

Tonya

Today was the day I'd find out the sex of my baby and I was so excited. I got out of bed and headed to the bathroom so I could shower and do my other daily hygiene. After finishing up, I put on my clothes and put my hair up in a messy bun.

I checked on my mom who was still resting then walked downstairs to talk with her nurse and let her know I would be making her breakfast, so all she had to do was warm it up. After making breakfast and eating, I took my prenatal pill and headed out to my doctor's appointment.

I got there and thanked God there wasn't a lot of people inside. I signed my name and got my labels before I took a seat. I picked up a magazine about pregnancy as more pregnant women came in and some were with their unborn baby's father. I tried my best not to look at the happy couples, but I couldn't help myself. Before I could stare any longer, the doctor called my name and I got up and walked to the back.

Showing me to the ultrasound room, she told me to lay on the bed and lift my shirt up. I did as she instructed and waited for her as I got a call from Dijah.

"Dijah I'm already in the room, just come to room 237."

I hung up and laid there and a few more minutes later, my bestie came in smiling and exchanged smiles with the doctor as well then sat in a chair close to my bed.

"I'm sorry I'm late, I had to drive Jr. over to my sister's."

"You not late, I really just got back here."

"You okay?"

"Yes, I'm excited."

"You know what you want to have?" the doctor asked me as she pulled up the ultrasound on the TV and computer screen.

"No, it doesn't matter to me long as it's healthy," I said, smiling as she put the cold jelly on my belly.

I looked over at Khadijah who was all into the TV screen waiting to see the baby. She moved the handle around and my baby looked well developed with a big ass head, I waited patiently for her to take the pictures.

"You ready to find out the sex now?" she asked and I shook my head yes. I looked over at Dijah's emotional ass and her ass was really crying and shit.

"Dijah, I know you not crying?"

She wiped her tears and began smiling.

"I cannot believe you about to be a mother right now, I really love this."

I laughed at her emotional ass and so did the doc which caused her ass to laugh too.

"Alright, I almost got it."

The baby moved and began to jump, but finally let the doctor see.

"It's a girl, congratulations!" the doctor said to me as she took pictures of her for me to have.

Tears began coming down my eyes once the doctor handed me my ultrasound pictures. Once I was cleaned up, I headed to the front to schedule my next appointment then walked out of the building with Khadijah following me.

"It's okay, Tee. Trust me my tee-tee baby is going to be so spoiled."

I wiped my tears away and put the pictures up in my purse.

"I know, but it just hurts to know that I will be having a little girl and she's already going through what I went through without having a father."

"I feel you, but you got Yatta. Yatta could be her godfather, Tee. Don't stress about that right now, just know that little girl is coming into this world soon and she's going to be very loved and spoiled, okay?"

"I hear you," I told her as I got into my car, "thank you for coming to my appointment with me."

"You don't have to thank me, it's no problem at all."

"I will call you when I make it back home. I'm about to go to the store first to go stuff my face, this little girl hungry with her greedy self."

"Okay, just make sure you call me when you make it home."

"Okay."

I got in and watched Dijah walk to her car then I drove off to a nearby restaurant.

Khadijah

I walked over to my car and dug in my bag for the keys and that's when I felt a cold, steel piece in the middle of my back.

"Don't yell, don't scream, and don't say shit. Just find them keys and open the damn door."

I could tell by his voice that it was Kenny. I grabbed my keys, unlocked my car and got inside with my purse. Before I could close the door all the way, I was face to face with Kenny's no good ass.

"What do you want Kenny? Why the fuck you pull a gun on me for?"

"You missed me? I know you tired of that bitch nigga Yatta."

"Actually, I don't miss you and no, I'm not tired of my man and never will be."

He chuckled and placed the gun in his lap still holding it.

"I remember when you were saying the same shit about me."

"Yeah, well I was young and dumb. You weren't shit and still ain't shit."

I spat at him, causing him to back hand me so hard it felt like one of my front teeth fell out. None did, but blood started to leak from my mouth and I began crying.

"I want my motherfucking son, bitch. You got that bitch ass nigga around my boy knowing he killed his uncle, you a spiteful ass bitch."

I didn't even respond to him, I just held my busted mouth and cried. He grabbed the back of my head with his free hand and the other hand had the gun pointed to my face.

"I want you to bring my fuckin' son to me tonight I don't want to hear no ifs, ands, or buts about the shit. Do you fuckin' understand me!"

"Kenny he don't even—"

Before I could get the words out, he smacked me again, causing me to hold my eye.

"I didn't ask for shit else but okay. Now do I make myself clear?"

I shook my head yes and he threw a piece of paper at me.

"This is the address you bring him to. Don't try no goofy shit because I will find you and I will kill you, bitch."

He got out of my car and I lifted my head up, reaching in the back for paper towels to wipe the blood off my hands and busted lip. After I did that, I drove back home and dialed Yatta's number.

"Hey baby."

"Yatta he's going to kill me!"

"Who? Where you at?"

"Kenny! I just made it home. I don't know how he knew where I was, but I had just watched Tee leave from her doctor's appointment and as I was getting ready to get in my car, he came up behind me with a gun. We got in the car and he hit me in my mouth and eye, he wants me to bring Jr. to him tonight!"

"Baby I'm on my way. Don't go nowhere and make sure you lock all the doors. I'm on my way!"

"Okay."

I went straight to the bathroom to clean around my mouth and when I looked in my mirror I did not like what I saw. My bottom lip was busted and my left eye had a mark under it turning black. After cleaning my face, I called my sister and let her know what happened and told her to keep Jr. with her a little while longer. She let me speak to him and he sounded like his normal, happy self so that lifted me up some.

Feeling helpless, stressed, and paranoid, I started to go in Yatta's stash to roll up but I decided against it, so I went down stairs to grab a cocktail. I made it back to the room and right as I heard Yatta slam the door. I walked to the stairway balcony to see he was making his way up the steps with his crutches. When he made it up the stairs, he immediately hugged and kissed me before examining my face.

I could tell he was beyond pissed by the fire in his eyes. He walked to the room and I followed behind him.

"Baby I want you to stay here and don't leave, okay?"

"Yeah, but I don't want you doing anything stupid."

"Well it's too late for that."

"Yatta just promise me you'll be safe and come back to me tonight, please?"

We looked into each other's eyes then he lightly grabbed my face and kissed me with so much love and passion I felt it was a goodbye kiss. He made his way over to the closet and got his gun and bullets and walked out the house. All I could do was pray he makes it back safe.

Jay

"So where do we find his bitch ass at?" I asked, sitting in the passenger's seat in Yatta's car blowing on some loud.

"That dumb ass nigga gave her the address so we gone head there and blow his ass the fuck down."

"True, I like the sound of that."

I began smoking the rest of the blunt and my phone flashed indicating I had a text message. I opened it and Tonya had sent me a text. Messing around with her ass was like a game of hot and cold, so I just gave her space.

Tonya: Hey Jay.

Me: What's up, how you been?

I'm not even going to front and say I'm not feeling her, but she gave me mixed signals about her feelings for me. She texted back but I ignored it because the car came to a stop.

"What the fuck type of house is this?"

"This shit look like a trap spot."

I looked around and the night was approaching. Looking at the spot I noticed the door was wide open.

"You see that shit?"

"Hell yeah."

"Go around back and I will get the front."

"A'ight, lets go."

We got out and I walked to the back of the place and Yatta went to the front. Keeping my gun right to my side, I pushed the door gently and it was open.

I walked in holding my gun up and I saw Yatta as I walked from the kitchen and up some stairs. Searching through the rooms, I saw pictures of Kenny and some kids with a big bitch so I assume this is where they lived. After coming up with nothing, Yatta and I met back out front and got in the car.

"They ass was not in there, bro," I said as Yatta drove off.

"His ass lives in a trap, that shit crazy. But he trying to get custody of Jr."

Yatta shook his head as he continued to drive.

"Hell yeah, that shit nasty. Did you see the fuckin' rooms?"

"Hell yeah I seen that nasty ass shit, but what's pissing me off more is one, his ass lives in a trap. Two, his ass put his fucking hands on Dijah. And three, this motherfucker wanted her to come there with Jr. Fuck type of shit he on man?"

I could tell Yatta was heated and I knew one thing for sure, he was going to get Kenny's ass and it was no stopping him. Dropping me off at the crib without a word, Yatta drove back home. I walked in my house and changed my clothes.

I picked up my phone and called Tonya.

"Hello?"

"Hey how you doing?"

"I'm fine, what about you?"

"I'm good. You free tonight?"

"Yeah, I'm free."

"You want to come over my place for the night? You know, watch movies and get to know each other better?"

"Yeah, that sounds good."

"Okay, I'm on my way."

"You just knew I was gone say yeah huh?"

I could hear her smile over the phone after she said it and I laughed.

"Just say I know how you feel about me."

The line got quit.

"Well I'm going to be on my way, so I will see you soon."

"Okay."

After brushing my waves a couple of times, I grabbed my jacket and walked out. I spotted Tonya sitting on the porch when I pulled up and began smiling. I was in daze watching her hips and thick thighs stroll over and climb into the car.

"You look beautiful."

"Thanks, you don't look bad yourself."

"So what movies you like to watch?" I asked as I pulled off.

"Drama and horror."

"Ah ok, so you like the scary movies huh?"

"I love those movies, I don't even get scared."

"We will see about that."

"What you want to eat?"

"We can get pizza and some snacks."

"Okay, cool."

Stopping at Pizza Hut, I grabbed us an extra-large, half cheese, half meat lovers' pizza then went to the corner store to grab some snacks for us along with some drinks. Arriving at my spot, I parked in the driveway and grabbed all the bags including the pizza and handed Tonya the keys.

She opened the door and I sat the food down on the table.

"Um, this not the same place u took me to the first time."

"I know, but this is my actual house."

"I guess."

I looked at her face and she sat down rubbing her stomach.

"I'm a single man, in case you thinking I'm on some other shit with you."

"Okay."

I sat next to her after grabbing the two plates and filled them both with slices of pizza. I turned on my Netflix and browsed the drama section first while taking bites of pizza.

"You should watch that one."

"Which one?"

"Just another girl on the irt."

"I never seen this before," I told her as I turned the movie on. "Did you find out what you were having?"

"It's a girl," she said smiling and I couldn't help but admire her beauty.

"Congratulations."

"Thank you."

"So do you have everything for her? Is it something you need?"

"I'm good on the clothes side and Dijah's supposed to help me with the pampers and everything else."

"I'm still going to get little mama some things."

"I appreciate it."

"It's no problem."

We watched the movie and ate. Times like this was always what I wanted. I really like Tonya and I was never going to leave her or baby girl's side.

Chapter Twenty-Four

Kenny

"Baby pass my blunt," I said to my girlfriend, Iesha. I began hitting the blunt then she started talking to me.

"Why haven't you got Jr. yet?"

"I'm going to get him, it's just going to take some time."

Iesha has two boys and they both were close in age, two and three. I met her around the time I got Dijah pregnant and me and her been kicking it hard since. Our living arrangements were going to change soon as I get Yatta and his homeboy out the way.

They ass killed my brother, therefore it was my honor to get their asses and take their money. As far as Khadijah, I still had feelings for her but she's too busy messing around with that fake ass nigga that ain't about shit.

"Well the kids aren't here so what you want to do?"

Iesha is a thick ass, brown skin chick. I fell in love with her heart and I made it my mission to do as I promised and get us out of this abandoned ass house.

"Shit we can do whatever you want baby."

Iesha got up and dropped her pants and underwear quick. She walked over to me and undressed me too. Just when she was about to fit all of me in her mouth, my phone began ringing.

"What's up?" I said, moving Iesha out the way.

"Fuck you mean a new nigga?"

"A'ight, I'm on my way."

I got up and put the blunt out then put my clothes back on.

"Baby I will see you later, some shit just popped up I got to handle."

"Okay, that's cool."

I got out the house and drove my beat up car over to my boy Johnny's place.

Arriving, I got out and knocked on the door and he answered.

"Yeah bro, I was saying it's a new nigga in town and he up there with Yatta on the money tip."

"When you hear this shit?"

"Today bro, as soon as I heard it I called you."

"Okay, that's no problem. We can just take his ass out now since he's new, and leave Yatta and Jay for last."

"Okay, when you want to do the shit?"

"This weekend, we need to get it done as soon as possible."

"A'ight, I got you bro."

I walked back out to my car and decided to just drive around and smoke to keep my mind on ease. I knew I'm going to take these niggas out and will be the next street king, I just had to get everything in order and plan my shit out carefully.

Yatta

It's been a couple of weeks since I got shot in my leg and it was healing up pretty good so I didn't need those damn crutches. I laid low until my leg healed because when I catch Kenny, I'm going to beat his ass like I'm his daddy after that shit he did to Dijah. The shit was not over with at all.

"Baby, I'm not feeling good."

"What's wrong?"

"I feel sick."

I looked at Dijah as she laid in the bed with Jr. He has been under her a lot lately.

"When was your last period?"

"A month ago, but it's probably coming late this month."

"Nope, I doubt it. You're pregnant," I said with confidence and she looked at me with not so happy eyes.

"Look baby, I'm going to go meet up with Jay real quick. Do you want me to pick you up a test?"

"You can, but why you leaving out so early?"

"I got shit to handle."

"Okay."

We kissed and I rubbed a sleeping Jr.'s head before I left out the house. Arriving at Jay's crib, Tonya came and answered the door with some pajamas on.

"What's up sis, Jay ready yet?"

"What's up, yeah he's finished."

Just when she stood back from the door, Jay walked out and gave her kisses on her lips and her stomach before we left.

"Damn, so you hitting that?"

"Nope, I'm just caring for her."

"Yeah right, nigga you know how much of a dog you are."

"It's not even like that. I really do like Tonya and I'm going to be there for her and baby girl."

"True, I hear you."

"So you finally found where this pussy nigga hiding at?"

"Hell yeah, I got information on where his ass at now."

Pulling up to Kenny's hide out, I pulled out my gun and Jay did the same. We walked up and heard laughter and people talking, I checked the small window on the side and it was Kenny and some other nigga smoking a blunt.

"A'ight, you go in after me," I whispered to Jay as he nodded his head.

We busted in through the front door and these dumb ass niggas ain't even have no heat on them, just sitting there looking stupid. As I grabbed Kenny, Jay grabbed his buddy and we hauled they ass back into our car.

"Man come on, you know I don't mean you no harm man just let me go," Kenny pleaded as I threw him in the back right along with his friend.

Even though I wasn't trying to get blood in my car, I just said fuck it and shot Kenny in both his arms and did the same to his buddy. After hearing the screams and cries, Jay got in and I drove down to a warehouse I always used to torture my victims.

We arrived and Kenny was still crying for me to spare his life, but I wasn't hearing shit and he knew it. Dragging them both inside the warehouse, Jay cut the lights on and I pushed Kenny's ass in a chair and Jay did the same to his friend.

"Aye man, it don't even got to be like this. We could be team mates Yatta, you heard about the new nigga in town man? We could team up and get his ass."

I never turned around from setting up the chains I was about to put them in.

"What new nigga?" I asked him.

"This nigga name D.J. He just came from Atlanta, he be out south."

"How the fuck you hear about him?"

"My guy told me."

After finishing the chains, I put Kenny's hands in the chains and rolled them up so his feet were no longer on the ground and again, Jay did the same to his friend.

"Come on Yatta man!"

"Shut the fuck up! Yo ass wasn't saying that shit when you shot me in the leg, or when you called yourself threatening Dijah."

"I didn't mean it man, I didn't mean it!"

I let off shots to his legs and feet as he screamed out in pain.

"Then you try to take her son from her like she hasn't been there for that boy all his two years of living. Where the fuck was you when he just had his birthday party? Yo' ass ain't even call Khadijah, but you want custody right?"

I didn't let him get a chance to say anything, I just shot him twice in between the eyebrows and did the same to his friend.

"Have the crew clean this shit up."

After Jay called the cleanup crew, we walked back to my car.

"Now that's out the way, what's that shit he was talking about a new nigga name D.J.? You heard of that nigga?" I asked Jay as I pulled off.

"Naw, I haven't heard of him, but I'm sure niggas around have. Shit we used to be the first ones to know shit."

"Hell yeah, we gone body his ass next. Coming in our city trying to make some money, he got us fucked up."

Jay nodded his head and I dropped him off back at home. Since it was still early, I traded my BMW for a new one but a different color which was grey. Driving back home, I got in the shower and dressed in a white tee and jogging pants. I walked into my computer room and put in the name D.J. in my search bar.

The nigga didn't look familiar at all and I was going to make it my goal to find this nigga and body his ass quick. I walked into the room with Dijah and Jr. and began drifting off to sleep with them holding on to Dijah.

Chapter Twenty-Five

D.J.

Walking to the store, I grabbed me a pack of blunts so me and my homies could roll up. Chicago was new to me and I was down here to dodge niggas down in Atlanta. Money wasn't a problem for me, so I moved myself into this big ass mansion soon as I got out here. All my life all I been doing was getting money. I had females here and there, but I never actually had a girlfriend.

I wasn't looking for one right now, all that was on my mind was making more money. When I got back to the house I rolled up a few blunts and my homies did the same, then we began to smoke. As I went to light my second blunt, my phone rang.

"Hello?"

"Why haven't you called me D.J.?"

"I been busy."

"Okay, so when are you going to let me visit you?"

"When I get settled and familiar with the city."

"Okay."

I hung the phone up on her. Lex was a female I use to fuck with hard, but I never gave her a chance to be my girl because I just wasn't ready.

"So how we gone compete with these Chicago niggas Dee?"

"Shit, personally, I'm not in competition. I just want to stack this money and live good out here."

"Yeah, but you know these niggas is crazy out here."

"I don't give a fuck, as long as nobody messing up me making my money then we straight."

"True."

We all chilled as we listened to music and smoked. Right about now might be good for lady friend, but I can't really trust these Chicago females so I would just lay low on that.

Khadijah

"Girl, you shouldn't even be up here," I said to Tonya as she started her clients head.

"I'm only six months. I can still work, calm down."

"Yeah, okay."

I walked back to the bathroom but I was done working for the day because my body was not feeling it, so I just clocked out early. Heading home, I checked up on Jr. at my sister's and then straight home wanting to surprise Yatta.

Walking into the house, I closed the door and walked up the stairs. I head moaning coming from my bedroom, so I walked in and there was Yatta's no good ass fucking on a thot bitch.

"Who the fuck is this Yatta!" I yelled, causing him to jump up from her looking at me crazy.

"What happened to you not going to hurt me no more? You know what, last fucking strike. Don't think about contacting, me it's over!"

"Baby it's not even like that, I brought her back from the shop—"

"That's what we on now? Bringing random bitches in our home and bed!"

Tears started to roll down my face and I just walked out feeling the urge to throw up. Yatta tried grabbing me but I just kept walking and drove off on his ass. I couldn't stop myself from crying. How could I be so fucking dumb to think he wasn't going to cheat again, he even brought the bitch home early thinking I was at work.

I pulled up at a hotel and checked in. Once I was settled in, I cut my phone on silent after checking on my baby boy one last time. I began to play music since it was usually the only thing that could make me feel better. After crying for damn near an hour, I got up and walked to the ice machine and I bumped into a tall, dark skin guy whose diamond earring shined in the sun.

"I'm sorry, beautiful," the guy said as he helped me up.

"It's no problem."

I walked up to the ice machine and I could feel his eyes staring at me, so I walked back to my room with the cup of ice not filled how I wanted it to be.

After eating majority of the ice, I began to drift off to sleep but that came to an end when I heard knocking at my door.

When I answered it was the dude from earlier, standing in front of me.

"Hey again, my name is D.J. Yours?"

"Dijah."

"Well it's nice meeting you Dijah."

He shook my hand and I couldn't help but get lost in his eyes.

"Me and my boys are having a hotel party, you want to join?"

"No, I don't do hotel parties."

"Well that's cool, I was just asking."

"Okay."

He started to say something else, but I closed the door on him and laid back down. My heart was hurting right now and I had no one to share my problems with, so I just cried until I got a headache and drifted to sleep.

The next morning, I got a call from Kesha saying the shop was closed today so I jumped in the shower and put on the clothes I had stashed in my bag. I grabbed my belongings and left out of the hotel. Just when I was about to get in my car, D.J. popped up again. Although he was fine, he was starting to work my nerves.

"How you doing this morning, beautiful?"

"I'm fine."

"I know you are, where you headed?"

"None of your business."

He laughed but I was dead serious.

"It's cool, I understand. I just wanted to speak to your beautiful ass this morning."

"Okay."

I drove off and headed over to Angel placed so I could pick my son up.

"What's up with you?" she asked me as I grabbed Jr. from her and placed him in his seat.

"It's just a lot going on right now, but I will be okay."

"You sure sis?"

"Yes, I'm sure."

"Okay, I will take your word for it this time."

I got in my car and drove over to my mother's and she let me in.

"Baby, what's wrong?"

"I'm going to go apartment hunting and I came over to ask you if you knew any good ones?"

"Yeah, you can put sleeping little man on that couch and come with me."

I put Jr. down and walked to the backroom with my mother and she sat at the computer while I sat in a chair next to her.

"You want a two bedroom, right?"

"Yes."

"And a two bathroom?."

"Yeah ma, just like the one I just had."

I held my head back and pushed my hair out of my face. I saw my mom look over at me as she scanned the information across the computer.

"What happened with you and Yatta?"

"He cheated, ma," I said feeling the tears leave my eyes and my face getting hot, which caused my mother to focus all of her attention on me.

"Baby, look at me."

I turned my head towards her and she came closer to me in the chair.

"I know you're hurting right now, but baby if that's the man you really love and want to be with then running isn't going to solve the problem."

"I know that ma, but this is not his first time and this time he had the chick in our house and in our bed! He promised me he wasn't going to cheat anymore, ma. What does it mean when a man constantly cheats after begging to get you back and promising that he's going to change?"

"I can take a guess, maybe he's scared of commitment. He wants to be with you, but he's probably afraid to be with you one hundred percent."

"I don't understand why he would be. I mean, we were doing good so I'm just confused and hurt right now."

"Well I say give it a couple of days, and after that y'all need to have a civil talk about the relationship."

I shook my head no meaning I was done with him. If he could do some foul shit like that to me, he never really cared and I was not going back. In the back of my mind I know I still love him, but I don't think him and I are going to work.

After my mom looked me up an apartment close to my old one, I headed out of the house, leaving Jr. so I could go rent it and buy the belongings I needed. If starting over at a new place with new things was what it took to be over the situation, then I was ready.

Unique

"You have three more months left, you need to stay off your feet and not eat as much salt because your blood pressure is a bit high," the doctor said to me as she took my blood pressure and wrote everything down in her notebook.

"Okay, so what if my blood pressure doesn't change before they're ready?"

"Then we would have to induce you before your due date."

I was excited to meet my babies already and three months was a long time from now.

"Other than that, everything looks okay. The babies are doing fine and I won't be seeing you again until next week to check on you blood pressure, so remember what I just told you."

"Okay, thanks a lot doc."

I got off the patient bed and walked to the front to schedule my next appointment. After I finished, I walked to the waiting area where Tasha was sitting and we got up and left.

"What did they say?"

"They are okay, but my blood pressure was a little high."

"Okay, so my god babies should be arriving in three months, right?"

"Yeah, if I can keep my blood pressure down."

"Well you just have to work on that."

"Yeah, I know."

We headed home and I was ready to get in my bed and head to sleep since Nick wasn't picking up to give me more information on Yatta. I really do miss him, so I canceled out any negative thoughts about having him killed because at the end of the day, I know he and I will be back together raising our babies.

Shatavia

Yatta

I sat in my bed all day not wanting to go anywhere. I haven't slept since the day Dijah left the house. She wasn't picking up her phone then got her number changed which passed me off.

I know I fucked up by bringing a bitch into our home and fucking her in our bed that we shared, but it's hurting me that she's just going on with life and not even caring for my explanation about the shit. My only choice was to go out looking for her.

I finally got out of the bed and headed to wash my ass. After my shower, I threw on some clothes and grabbed my coat. Hoping in my car I went to her mom's house first since it was the closest, but she wasn't there so I tried her sister's house and she wasn't there either. Feeling agitated, I grabbed my weed and blunt and began rolling up, but before I sparked my shit up I saw Dijah's ass laughing and giggling with some dark skin nigga.

I got out the car and made my over to their ass, holding the gun in the small of my back.

"Sorry to break this shit up but she got a man, so you can get the fuck out her face now," I said to dude who looked like he was no competition on the street side.

"That ain't what she told me."

I looked over at Dijah who was rolling her eyes at me in disgust.

"You telling niggas you single now!"

"You can leave now, I don't need no audience!" I said to dude once I noticed he wasn't leaving.

"Let's see what she says, do you want me to go Dijah?"

"No, you good. Let's just go somewhere else."

When she said that shit and tried to walk off, I yanked her ass by her neck. She had me fucked up if she thought she was about to diss me in front of this nigga.

"Let me the fuck go Yatta!"

"Get yo' ass in the car!"

"Aye, I will holla at you later Dijah!"

"You won't be talking to shit later fam. I suggest you shut the fuck up if you know what's good for you!"

He walked off with a smirk on his face and this nigga was lucky I was not in the mood right now. My only concern was Khadijah and getting her back. When she got in the passenger side, she slammed the door and folded her arms across her chest.

"Man what the fuck you change your number on me for? Then you out with that nothing ass nigga, fuck is up?"

"You already know what's up, I'm not with you."

"You're still my woman so you not single, so stop saying that shit."

I couldn't resist the fact her ass was looking sexy as fuck in the black high waist pants with her brown UGG boots and Victoria's Secret coat on with her hair straightened.

"No, I am single. I gave you another chance and you fucked up big time. Ain't no coming back from that, period."

"I'm sorry, baby."

She didn't even look at me she was staring off looking outside the window.

"I know I fucked up, but I'm just not ready right now Dijah. I know I said I was, but I just want you by my side and I swear I will stop these childish ass games."

"Yeah, you said the same shit last time. I'm not wasting my time with you no more, all you had to do was say that shit in the beginning and I wouldn't've put my feelings into this shit."

I saw tears coming down her face and tried to wipe them, but she just pushed me away.

"Dijah, look at me."

"I know what I did was wrong on many levels, but baby I'm coming to you. I'm being a man about this shit. I'm telling you from this point on, I'm not on that shit. It don't make me feel better."

"So why you keep doing it Yatta?"

"I was just seeing if it was going to make any difference, but it don't. I want you nobody else, baby. I want you and Jr. to come back so we can be a family again."

I waited to see a reaction out of her but I didn't get it. She looked at me with her grey eyes.

"I can't Yatta."

Those words shattered my heart, but It made me realize how much hurt I caused her.

"Dijah, I love you. I just need you to forgive me and let me start over this time."

"I can't Yatta, I thought you were serious the first time you said the shit. I just need time to myself right now."

I nodded my head and let her exit the car and walk to hers before she drove off. I sparked my blunt up and began driving with no destination in mind. I just needed to clear my head, so I turned my radio up to the 90's R&B station as I smoked and drove around.

Chapter Twenty-Six

Two months later...

Khadijah

    Things been going okay for me since my break up with Yatta, but I still miss him. I just can't be in that position where he keeps cheating thinking everything will be fine afterwards. I decorated my new apartment to my liking, bought new TV's, furniture, and beds, and of course household items. I still was good on the money side because I worked at the salon in the morning and at night I was back at the club.

    Jr. was straight and kept asking me about Yatta, but I just tell him he's away at work. Getting up preparing breakfast for me and my son to get the day started, I put on my shorts and tank top and checked on Jr. first.

    As I was getting things ready in the kitchen, there was a knock at the door so I walked over to check the peep hole. Opening up, I let him in and gave him a hug.

"What's been going on, Dijah?"

"Nothing, getting breakfast ready for my son and I."

"Why you been avoiding me?"

"I'm just not ready to talk to nobody on that level D.J."

"I get that, but you can't talk to me on a friend level?"

"I don't have time for male friends."

"Well we been texting and calling each other, why stop?"

"I just told you."

He sat down on my couch while I started cooking. In the middle of making the food, he got up from his seat and came over and hugged me from the back making me put down the pan.

"You need to stop playing with me and give me a chance, baby."

The words he whispered into my ears had me on ten, but I had to be strong and not some easy chick he's used to.

"D.J. I will catch up with you later."

"Okay, just hit my line."

"Okay, I got you."

Walking him to the door I opened it, and when he got on the other side of the door he turned to me looking at me with his dark brown eyes.

"I hope you not kicking me out."

We both laughed and I shook my head.

"No, I just got things to do today, but I promise I'll catch up with you later."

"Okay beautiful."

I closed the door and finished making breakfast for Jr. and I. We ate and I gave him a bath and got him dressed so I could drop him off at Angel's. After I dropped him off, I raced back home to get dressed for work.

Making it there on time, I clocked in and already had a client waiting on me.

"Good morning Keisha."

"Good morning girl."

I walked over to my station and set up my things and told my customers to sit in the chair.

Two hours later I was done with my first head and was super hungry, so I took my break. I spotted Yatta looking at me, but I just ignored him and proceeded to get in my car. Soon as I unlocked the doors he raced to the passenger side and got in, causing me to roll my eyes.

"What's up Khadijah, long time no talk."

"Yeah, I know."

"Where you headed too?"

"To get lunch, why?"

"Just asking, you mind if I join you?"

"I don't care."

I pulled off figuring out the nearest restaurant to go to.

"You know word gets back to me quick, right?"

"I don't care about anybody's word."

"Well you should, how you gone be pregnant with my baby but still stripping and shit."

"I'm not pregnant."

I pulled the car over in an empty parking lot and kept looking out my review mirror.

"Fuck you mean you not pregnant?"

"I had a miscarriage Yatta."

The car got silent and I tried so hard not to cry in front of him, but I had no choice. When I moved out and got settled in my place I went and visited the doctor's office and I found out I was three months, but a week later I miscarried due to stress that I tried not to do.

"What happened Dijah?"

I wiped my face and looked at him.

"I found out I was three months when I left and a week later, I miscarried due to stress. All I did was kill my baby Yatta, stressing over shit you did! I wanted to share the news about being pregnant so bad, but my pride wouldn't let me. I just cried and stressed when I should have been happy about my second baby."

I watched as he looked at me with tears in his eyes and it made more fall from mine.

"Drive back to the shop."

"I have to get my lunch Yatta."

"Just drive back to the shop."

I wiped my tears and drove back to the shop which wasn't far from where we were. Yatta got out and walked to the driver's side, opening my door pulling me out.

"What are you doing?"

He didn't say a word, but he directed me to his car and we got in and he drove in the direction of his house.

"Why are we going here?"

"I need to talk to you about some shit."

"You know I have to work Yatta, it could wait."

"I will tell Keisha you was with me you, will be straight."

I sat quietly in my seat and my phone began ringing. I clicked the end button because it was D.J. The whole ride to the house he was blowing up my phone and I could tell Yatta was getting pissed off. When we arrived, I got out and followed him up the steps and into the house.

When we made it to the bedroom, my phone rung once more and he snatched it and answered it.

"Aye motherfucker, you already don't belong here. Don't make me have your time ending early, stop calling my girl phone!" Yatta yelled into the phone then hung it up and passed it back to me.

"You getting yo' number changed just like you changed yo' shit on me."

I just looked at him and didn't say anything as he sat down on the bed.

"You not going to sit next to me?"

I made a stank face.

"Last time I was here you was fucking some bitch on this bed, so no I'm good."

"Dijah the sheets been changed and no other female been in this bed since so sit down."

I sat down and put my head in my hands and he just moved them out of my lap so I was facing him.

"You had to go through that miscarriage alone with our baby. I admit to my fuck ups and I'm sorry baby, but let's move forward please because I want to be the one apart of you and Jr.'s life."

"Yatta, I'm not even trying to be in a relationship right now."

"I know I fucked up, but baby I promise there will be no more of that shit."

I shook my head because I heard this line twice from him and I just didn't know what to think anymore.

"What's supposed to be different Yatta?" I asked curious to know his response.

"I'm going to do my best and I won't even look at another female baby, I just want you and only you."

I looked into his eyes to see if he was telling me what I wanted to hear, or sincere about his apology, but I could see some sincerity.

"I'm not about to be going back and forth with you, Yatta. This is my life and I don't deserve how you keep playing with my feelings."

"I know, Dijah and my fuck ups are not what you deserve. I know and I plan on doing it the right way from this point on. I told you I want to start a family, I want to live like them white people you see on TV."

"It all sounds good until you slip and fuck another bitch."

He got off the bed and got on his knees in front of me while grabbing my face lightly so we were eye to eye.

"I don't want another girl, I don't need another girl. All I want and need is you, what do I have to do to make you see that?"

"I don't know Yatta, all I know is I'm tired of being hurt."

"And I'm going to fix it baby, I promise."

"I still need time to myself though."

"How much time is that?"

"A couple of more weeks. I'm still pissed about the shit and I really don't want to be here because of what the fuck I saw last time."

"Where you been staying?"

"In an apartment."

"Where at?"

"I'm not telling you all that."

"You should so I could know if it's a safe area or not."

"I been over there for two months, nothing's happened yet so I'm good."

"What about me dropping you off?"

"You can take me back to the salon."

Yatta got up and walked towards the door pushing his dreads out his face.

"You ready to leave?"

"Yeah."

I got up and began walking towards the door and he grabbed me by my waist.

"I don't want you stripping, you already know that shit."

"I didn't want you cheating and you been knew that."

"You have a job so why would you go back stripping, Dijah?"

"Because I need the extra money to get the shit I want."

"I don't want you working up at no club man."

"I don't care Yatta, move out the way."

I began walking down stairs and he followed behind.

"I will give you some money. That's what you want, right?"

"I don't need your money."

"You think I want other niggas to see my girl butt ass naked, shaking ass, and showing pussy for money?"

I just stood and stared at him not giving a damn what he had to say because he didn't have a say so in what the fuck I do.

"You going backwards, Dijah."

"Yatta, just take me back to the shop."

He let out a long sigh before opening the door and taking one last look at me and we got in the car and headed back to the salon.

"What about my food? You just made me miss lunch."

"I got you."
I could tell he was pissed off, but I didn't give a fuck. He should have thought about the outcome before he stuck his dick in the next bitch. Now he thinks he's going to control what the fuck I'm doing, he needed to think about something else because I wasn't changing shit about what I was doing. Besides, it takes the stress away from me at the end of the day.

Unique

He's a Bad Boy but I Love Him

I woke up out my sleep to a sharp pain and I pulled the covers back to see that I was lying in a puddle of water. I began to panic as I screamed for Tasha, but her ass probably left after I went to sleep. I called the ambulance and they said they would be on the way. I made it out of the bed and winced in pain and called Yatta's phone. *It's two in the morning so he probably won't answer,* I thought to myself as his phone rung.

"Hello?"

"Yatta, I'm going to the hospital. I'm in labor," I said in between contractions.

"Okay, what hospital you going to?"

"They're taking me to UI."

"Okay, just call me when you make it so I can know which room and floor."

"Okay."

I hung up and grabbed my babies' hospital bags and got downstairs the best way I could. When I got to the door, the ambulance was pulling up with sirens ringing. I locked up and two EMT ladies helped me into the ambulance.

When I arrived, they wheeled me into the labor and delivery part and hooked me up to a machine so they could monitor my babies' heart beats. After the doctor checked my cervix, they told me I was five cementers and they moved my bed to a big hospital room with a TV.

"Okay, my name is Tiana and I'm going to s your nurse for the night," a brown skin, tall lady said as she wrote her name on the board.

"Is there anything you need?"

"Just some ice, thank you."

259

The nurse smiled and she walked out to get me some ice. I picked up the phone and dialed Yatta's number.

"Yeah, I'm up here. What's the room number?"

"It's 303, labor and delivery."

"A'ight."

Yatta hung up the phone and I put mine down. I was now calm that Yatta would be by my side; even though he doubted that the twins were his, I respect him for coming. He walked in with a slight smile as he pulled a chair close to my bed and it made me smile too.

"What's up, what are they saying?"

"I'm five centimeters now."

"It goes up to ten, right?"

"Yeah."

I watched Yatta look around the room then he looked at the monitor that was making a beeping noise indicating the babies' heart beats. Looking at him had me feeling the way I felt about him when were teenagers all over again. He looked so sexy with his dreads braided to the back and his mustache was neatly trimmed, bringing out his sexy features.

"So you still doubting they are yours?"

"I just want the DNA done."

I nodded my head as I flicked through the channels trying to find something interesting to watch. From the corner of my eye I could see Yatta texting on his phone, but from the look of it I can tell he's sad or mad about something.

"Everything's okay?"

"Yeah, I'm good. What about you?"

"I'm go— Ahhh!"

Yatta got out of his chair and stood up over me with a worried look.

"What's wrong, you need a doctor?"

"No, it's just contractions. They hurt like hell, I'm probably going to get an epidural in a minute."

Yatta sat back down then continued texting on his phone, and I just laid on one side of the bed trying to fight these contractions.

Chapter Twenty-Seven

D.J.

"Bro I will be back, I'm about to go make some moves real quick."

"A'ight, you got yo' heat on you?"

"You already know I do, bro."

I walked out and was headed over to Dijah's crib early in the morning. It's something about her that drives me crazy on the inside. Getting in my car, I drove about ten minutes before arriving at her spot. I walked up some steps and rung her doorbell with a smile on my face.

"What the fuck D.J.?"

"Damn, you not surprised to see me?"

"It's six in the morning and if my son was here I would curse you the fuck out for ringing my bell this damn early in the morning."

"You gone let a nigga freeze to death?"

She let me in and shut the door before she walked to her couch and laid down, so I sat by her foot.

"Why you keep playing with me Dijah?"

"What do you mean?"

"I mean why won't you give me a chance?"

"I told you why, for the hundredth time already D.J."

"I know that, but our chemistry seems to tell me otherwise."

Dijah was looking sexy as hell in her silk robe and it had me wondering if she had anything on up under it, so I moved closer to her.

"I'm just not ready for no relationship right now."

"How many times you gone tell me that? Nothing wrong with me being your friend."

I rubbed my hand up her thigh and she sat up removing it.

"I don't do friends with benefits either."

"So when you think you can give me a chance then?"

"I don't know y—"

Before she could finish her sentence, I kissed her soft plump pink lips and we stared at each other until she got up.

"You need to leave."

"Come on baby, you know you want me as bad as I want you. I'm not on no other shit, you the one for me, real talk."

"I've heard that shit so many times it don't even faze me no more."

"Listen to me baby doll, I'm nothing like them other niggas you fucked around with. I'm as real as it gets and when I know what I want I pursue it until it's all mine."

Whispering the last words in her ear, I started to kiss her ear lobe causing her to moan a little. We locked eyes again and her eyes were the sexiest, hypnotizing, beautiful eyes I ever seen; I never had a girl whose eyes changed colors.

We kissed and this time our tongues danced around in each other's mouth's as we walked down the hall to her bedroom. Undressing myself I pulled out my magnum and she took her robe off answering my suspension that she was naked. I gently pushed her on the bed and climbed on top of her sucking on her nipples while I slipped my finger in her wet box.

Hearing her moans turned me on, so I put the condom on and slowly put my ten-inch manhood inside of her.

"You okay?" I asked her while I slowly stoked her, trying to fit all of me in her.

She just nodded her head and I put my head in the crook of her neck and began sucking on it. I could tell she was shy, so I continued to suck on her neck until she felt comfortable and began going in and out of her.

"Oh my God!"

I heard her say as I hit her spot. Now that I've found it, I was hitting it with every long stroke I gave her until she was clawing at my back. Then, I went deeper causing her nails to dig in my back, but I was liking that shit.

"D.J. I'm about to cum!"

I lifted my head up so we were face to face, looking at each other and her body began shaking underneath me letting me know she had climaxed, and a few seconds later I joined her.

Getting off of her I laid next to her and noticed she had tears falling from her eyes when I looked at her.

"What's wrong Dijah?"

"I don't want to talk about it, it's nothing."

"You know you could talk to me about it."

She wiped her tears and got out the bed and grabbed her robe to put it back on.

"I know that, I just don't want to."

I got up and took the condom off then threw it away before I put my clothes back on.

"Everything's going to be okay, whatever you're crying about. If you want to discuss it later I'm all ears."

"Okay."

I watched as she led me to the front and opened the door so I could walk, out but I turned to face her before she could close the door.

"I will call you soon as I get home, okay?"

She nodded her head and I kissed her lips one more time and hugged her before walking away. The whole ride home had me confused. I didn't understand why she was acting the way she was, she had me feeling like my sex game was weak. I know for a fact that couldn't be it, so I just flamed up a pre-rolled blunt and let my speakers bleed the rest of the drive home.

Tonya

Getting up, I noticed Jay was gone so I decided to take a shower and get dressed. Being eight months was stressful as hell. My belly grew more than my body and I could not wait 'til I have her because I was walking around looking like a balloon stick and that was not what's up.

Leaving out I made a stop to grab me some breakfast. Getting out, I waddled my way into McDonald's and surprised this motherfucker was packed and drive-thru was too, so I just took a seat at one of the tables and waited for the line to get smaller.

"Girl yes, that's word around town. That shit crazy," a dark skin girl said talking to her friend I'm guess.

I tried my best not to eat hustle and got on my phone to scroll down my Facebook timeline, but that didn't help.

"So he killed Chris and Kenny?"

"Yes, I heard that they were trying to rob him or some shit. That just goes to show you can't trust all your friends."

I rolled my eyes at the two gossipers and walked out before I said some shit to their asses. With my hormones, I know for a fact I was going to end up slapping at least one of them. I got in in my car and thought of other places in the area to grab something to eat from as my phone rung.

"Hey Dijah, how are you?"

"I'm not okay."

I heard her sobbing in between her words and I could instantly tell something was terribly wrong.

"Where are you?"

"I'm at home."

She managed to get out in between her crying.

"I'm on my way."

I raced over to my girl because never has she ever called me crying. Dijah was always the strong type, she would always try to be strong for me so it was my turn to do the same for her.

Getting there twenty minutes later, she opened the door for me and I sat on the couch next to her. She was looking a mess with her hair all over her head, her clothes were baggy, and her eyes were a dark grey color and she had puffy bags under them.

"What is wrong, Dijah?"

"I'm confused and I'm just hurt, Tee."

"What are you confused about?"

"I miss Yatta so much, but he cheated on me twice and I didn't want him to think he could continue to do that shit to me and everything would be fine. I talked to him the other day and he wanted me to come back home, but I told him no because I still needed my space which is true. So you remember the guy D.J. I was telling you about?"

"Yeah."

"We had sex this morning."

"Well Dijah it's nothing wrong with that. You didn't cheat, you're just exploring your options."

"I know, I liked it, but I feel it was too soon."

"Girl you will be okay, just keep that a secret. If you feel Yatta's not going to change, tell him. If you want to go back to him, don't tell him."

"But I like to be honest to him about stuff."

"Well to each its own, so you do what you feel like is best for you."

Dijah got up and hugged me then looked at me.

"I just needed an ear about my problems. I'm still confused on what to do, but I will figure something out," she said as she wiped her eyes with her sleeves.

"Dijah I will be here for you okay?"

"That's not all though."

"What you mean?"

"I had a miscarriage."

I grabbed my chest and stomach.

"When? Oh my God, Dijah!"

"Right when I moved out of Yatta's place and got settled here. They told it was due to me stressing, I was three months."

"Oh my God, I'm sorry to hear this. Why didn't you call me?"

She fell in my arms bawling her eyes out and I just rubbed her back still in shock at what she told me.

"Did you tell Yatta?"

"Yes, I told him when I saw him the other day and he was on that get back together shit, but I'm not ready yet. I miss his ass so much but I can't keep being easy for him."

"I feel you Dijah, everything is going to be okay."

"I really love Yatta's ass and I want to take his word when he says he's going to do right and be a family, but I can't keep being weak for him."

"Yeah, you always have to put your foot down at one point. Just take it easy, I've never seen you crying like this."

She got up and wiped her eyes and sat next to me.

"I'm sorry, I just had to let it out."

"It's no problem at all."

"How are you and my baby?"

"We're fine, I went to my doctor's appointment last week and they say she's doing good."

"One more month and baby girl will be here, did you figure out a name yet?"

"I'm stuck between Heaven and Cassandra."

"I like Heaven but Cassandra sounds like a good name too. Are you giving her your last name or Chris's?"

"My last name."

Right then and there I wanted to tell her what I heard up at McDonald's, but she's already hurt so I wasn't about to add to her pain.

"What did you have planned for the day?"

"Jr.'s staying at my mom's for a while and I'm just getting myself together."

"Well you don't want me to stay with you?"

"No. I'm okay. You heard enough of my problems," she said showing a weak smile.

"Well just call me over whenever you need me."

"Okay, thanks for listening to me Tee."

"It's okay."

I got up and walked to the door and Dijah was right behind me. We hugged before I left and went on about my day.

Yatta

I haven't slept since two in the morning and it was now the afternoon and I was waiting for Unique to get out of surgery. One of the baby's heart beat was dropping so they rushed her into the surgery room to get a C-section.

My mind was all over the place, I thought about the babies possibly being mine and back to not having the love of my life, Khadijah by my side. As I got up to stretch, a male doctor came walking towards me with a smile on his face.

"Are you the father of Ms. Nick's babies?"

"I don't know yet," I answered honestly.

"Well they are here and they are a set of beautiful, happy, and healthy twins."

"So are they both going to be okay?"

"Yes, everything went well. You can go see them in the nursery down the hall and make a left."

"Okay, thanks a lot."

"No problem, congratulations."

My heart was beating out of my chest as my legs walked down the hall. Thinking these could be my seeds had a bittersweet feeling inside of me. Arriving in the nursery, it was three babies in a room.

"Hello sir I need to read your wristband."

Walking over to the nurse, I pulled up my coat sleeve and showed her the information on the wrist band. She walked me over to the babies that information matched mine.

"These are your two right here."

She pointed to the two beds they were in and they were fast asleep, so I took my coat off and placed it on the back of the chair as I pulled up close to them and sat down.

When I sat and looked at them I couldn't help but picture my baby pictures and they were looking just like me, so I asked for the nurse to come over.

"I want a DNA test done on these two, asap."

"DNA testing results comes back within two weeks."

I pulled out a stack and she began setting up the items needed for testing. After swabbing my mouth then swabbing the babies mouths, I watched her walk out taking it to the lab. Waiting for the results, the boy woke up looking directly at me.

"Hey little man, how you doing?" I cooed to him and he smiled. Wanting me to pick him up, he began to fuss until I carefully got him up, making sure to hold his head.

"What's up boy?"

I held him on me and he was just looking around. Although this feeling was new to me, I loved it and felt a connection that he was mine.

I smiled and talked to him while his sister was sleeping then he began to cry when he saw one of the nurses.

"What's wrong, man? You want your bottle?"

She walked over to the bottles, grabbed one, and shook it before screwing the top on it.

"You want to feed him?"

"Yeah."

I sat in the chair and held him up as the nurse showed me how to feed him. This boy was only a few hours old and his little behind drunk half the bottle.

"You have to put him on your shoulder to burp him, or you can just sit him up and pat his back."

I sat him up and he instantly let out a big belch. I laughed to myself at how tiny he was but just belched like a grown man.

"What's up, big man. You was hungry, huh?"

He played with my hands as he looked at me. I picked him up and tried to lay him on me again, but he threw up all on my shirt.

"You just got me good little man," I said as I held him off me a little bit and the nurse grabbed him so I wiped myself down with the paper towels. After I finished, the nurse I paid for the rapid DNA walked in with an envelope and I took it from her. Not wanting to open it just yet, I grabbed my coat and stepped out into the busy hallway and opened it.

My eyes scanned down to both names and it said 99.9% for them both. At this moment my heart was screaming with joy, but at the same time saddened because my mother would never get to see my kids. She would never get to bake them cookies, spend time with them, or nothing.

I walked to Unique's room and she was on her phone but hung up.

"What's up, how you feeling?" I asked her.

"I'm fine, did you see the babies?"

"Yeah, they're beautiful and small."

"Yeah, I seen them when they cut them out."

"What are you naming them."

I looked at her as she looked down at her sheets.

"My baby girl's name is Tanisha and baby boy's name is Damarion."

"Where you get that name from?" I asked curiously.

"My late aunt Jewel."

"I want him to have my name and I want baby girl to have my lady name."

"You know they might not be—"

"They are, I had the test done already."

She had a look of relief on her face.

"Well you're going to have to be here to sign the birth certificates and everything."

"Okay, when is that?"

"Tomorrow."

"Okay, but I'm going to get up out of here to clean up and stuff. I'll be back tomorrow."

"Okay, be safe."

"Alright, you get some rest."

She nodded her head and I walked out and got into my car, headed over to Dijah's mothers house.

I had to make things right between us. I needed her back in my life so bad that it was hurting me and I couldn't think straight without hearing her voice, or making her laugh, or playing games with Jr.

Chapter Twenty-Eight

Yatta

Getting out of the car, I walked up to Dijah's mother's door and rang the doorbell. A few seconds later she opened the door.

"Hey Yatta, how are you?"

"I'm fine ma, yourself?"

"I'm doing alright, you want to come in?"

"Yes, thank you."

She stepped out of the way and I walked in as she closed the door. Sitting down on the couch I heard Jr.'s voice.

"So, what's going on?"

"I came to you to find out where Khadijah is."

I could tell by the look on her face that she knew exactly where she was, but was hesitant to tell me.

"She doesn't want me telling you where she lives."

"I understand that, but I can't live without her. I know what I've done to her was wrong and I want to make things up to her and let her know I'm serious about us."

She let out a sigh then sat next to me.

"Son look, you have to promise me one thing if I give you this address."

"Okay, what is it mama?"

"Promise me you're not going to cause my daughter anymore pain the way you did. She told me about the miscarriage and I was hurt for her, I know from experience how she feels about it. I want my daughter to be happy. She's been through a lot and all I want for her is to be happy."

"I understand, I got you mama. That's all I want for her too, but it's like now I can't go on without her, like I'm incomplete. I'm missing her bad."

"She just wants to teach you a lesson for hurting her. I like you and I feel you are the one for her, I see the sincerity in your eyes."

After she shot me a smile, Jr. came running in the room yelling daddy and jumped right in my arms as hugged me tight and I did the same.

"Daddy I missed you, where you been?" he asked looking like Dijah.

"I've been busy, but I promise I will be back to come and get you soon."

"Okay, my mommy is sad daddy."

Hearing him tell me that broke my heart. He wasn't used to seeing her sad and hurting before and I know that's why she had him over here.

"Look at me Jr."

He looked up into my eyes.

"Mommy's going to be okay, she and daddy will make sure if it."

He nodded his head and got down.

"Grandma can I have cookie?"

"You sure can, granny man."

I watched as she got up and headed to the kitchen to give him a cookie and walked back into the room. After giving me her address, I thanked her and kissed Jr. bye before I got in my car driving over to the address I was given.

Pulling up, I got out and walked up a few steps and rung the doorbell for the second floor.

I saw her look out the window then open it.

"Why are you here Yatta?"

"I need to talk to you Dijah."

"I can't talk right now."

"Why is that? Let me in."

"I'm it letting you up."

Someone came out the front door and they held the door for me and I walked up to Dijah's door and began knocking.

"You might as well open this door or it's coming down straight up."

I heard the sound of locks being unlocked and when she opened the door, I barged my way in before she could stop me.

"Why are you here? I didn't call you to come over here."

"I need to talk to you about some shit."

I looked her over and saw a few hickies and realized she was walking around in a robe. The only time I knew she did that is when she's trying to fuck or already did.

Shatavia

"So you fucking somebody else now?"

"Look, don't be coming in here questioning me because you're not even supposed to be here Yatta."

Before I could curse her ass out, that nigga D.J. walked in from the back with his shirt off so I already know what was up.

"This the shit you do now!"

Feeling my blood boil I turned to dude getting ready to beat the fuck out of him.

"Didn't I tell yo' ass to stay the fuck away from her fam!"

Before he said anything, I punched him right in the jaw causing him to fall over. I went for my gun as he tried to swing back and I ducked, then hit him with the butt of my gun.

"I told yo' bitch ass to stay the fuck away from my girl, didn't I! And you fucked her!"

I hit him repeatedly with my gun then got up and grabbed Dijah by her arms as she cried for me to stop and leave.

"Why would you do this to me man?"

"You need to leave!"

"Why!"

"I don't owe you any explanation! Why did you do this to me? You pushed me to this point Yatta, I was nothing but a faithful, loving girlfriend to you so why? You answer that!"

Before I could say anything, I heard shots being fired and fell to the floor on top of her feeling pain in my back then looked at her and seen her mouth drop open as tears ran down her face.

278

"Yatta help me!" was all I heard her say as I blacked out, hoping we didn't die.

THE END!!!!

CPSIA information can be obtained
at www.ICGtesting.com
Printed in the USA
LVOW10s1527270417

532420LV00009B/798/P

9 781542 656863